Just the brush of skin against skin was enough to turn his belly upside down, his chest inside out.

Davis looked down at Violet, her cinnamon-brown eyes soft with an openness he hadn't seen since she'd returned. Questions, answers.

Could it work if we tried again?

Yes, he thought, in this moment. *Yes, it could.*

He could hear her breathing, and each inhalation swept through him, too. It seemed right to go a little further—to wind his finger around hers under the cover of all those ribbons, to link to her in such a small yet significant way.

Around them, it was as if everything and everyone had stopped motion, frozen in time while Violet and Davis caught up with each other in the Texas heat.

Kiss her. God, he wanted to kiss her so badly....

Dear Reader,

Welcome to my new Special Edition miniseries—
St. Valentine, Texas!

It's so exciting to settle in to a fresh town, especially one
that has a deeply buried secret that's about to unravel,
thanks to a stranger who sets off a series of events that
start in this book.

The two people who go about investigating this secret are
our hero and heroine, but digging up the town's past isn't
all they're doing—there's love in the air for them, in spite
of a painful, shared past of their own. But this Romeo and
Juliet are going to find a happy ending, no matter what
obstacles befall them!

Thanks so much for reading my books! In appreciation,
I always have a contest running at my website,
www.crystal-green.com. You can also check my blog
and Twitter (I'm @CrystalGreenMe) for updates about
my upcoming projects!

All the best,

Crystal Green

COURTED BY THE TEXAS MILLIONAIRE

CRYSTAL GREEN

Recycling programs
for this product may
not exist in your area.

ISBN-13: 978-0-373-65670-7

COURTED BY THE TEXAS MILLIONAIRE

CRYSTAL GREEN

lives near Las Vegas, where she writes for the Harlequin Special Edition and Blaze lines. She loves to read, overanalyze movies and TV programs, practice yoga and travel when she can. You can read more about her at www.crystal-green.com, where she has a blog and contests. Also, you can follow her on Facebook at www.facebook.com/people/Chris-Marie-Green/1051327765 and Twitter at www.twitter.com/ChrisMarieGreen.

To all you readers who have allowed me to write for you.
It's been over ten years now (!), and I hope the dreams
you find in these books are just as beautiful
as the ones you have in life.

Chapter One

Violet Osborne was back.

Davis Jackson watched her slow down as she walked by his newspaper office and peer through the glass window. He *lowered* his flute of champagne while, around him, the fundraiser he was hosting for the town's Helping Hand Foundation sparkled with activity, much like the Cristal bubbles in the drink he'd served to his guests.

Violet.

The girl who'd gotten away.

She stopped at his door. His heart thudded, as if it was running backward, fifteen years to the past, to the day she'd left him for college, abandoning little St. Valentine, Texas, in her rearview mirror. Abandoning him.

Their gazes locked as they stood there, and he knew she could feel everything he felt—the sharp edges of all the questions left unanswered between them, the tension of seeing each other again, all grown up, years later, man and woman.

Although Violet smiled at him, there were shadows in her brown eyes as she said hello by pressing her fingers to the glass that separated them.

Something clenched in Davis's chest, and he forgot that he was in a crowded room, full of the town's upper crust dressed in their cocktail-hour best.

Violet. Here.

The mayor's voice brought Davis back. "Dessert's ready!"

Davis heard everyone migrate toward the back of the high-tech office, toward where they'd pitched white tents outside to accommodate the food. Violet still waited, as if she didn't know whether to come inside or just walk away from Davis. Again.

The memory of that day, the slam of realizing that he didn't mean all that much to Violet, the miner's daughter he'd fallen for, the off-limits girl who'd seemed to know him better than anyone, tore into Davis like a fresh wound. But what pained the most was what she'd said that day, just before she'd left for college.

"Is it true? Are there other girls, Davis?"

Even though she'd said that she hadn't believed it when she'd heard it, he'd seen a different story in her eyes—a doubt that he hadn't changed enough to truly love her.

And that doubt had crushed the life out of what they'd had together in one swift moment, even if they'd naively thought nothing could tear them apart....

He opened the door, and Violet took a breath, as if she was readying herself for a reunion, not only with him, but with all the people who were filtering out of the back exit, checking her out and dismissing her because she was hardly important to them.

But Violet wouldn't have been expecting any fuss from the others—not after she'd spent her time in St. Valentine making it plain that she wanted to leave. The attitude hadn't gone over well with the townies *or* most of the miners.

Yet she'd made good on all her youthful confidence, hadn't she?

Her sophisticated hairstyle made her straight, dark red hair brush her neck. It went well with those big brown eyes that told you there was a quick mind always at work. Womanly curves, too, enhanced by a fashionable yet professional yellow summer blouse and white pants that hugged shapely hips and long legs…

Yeah, all grown up now.

"Violet," he said, and it sounded as if he'd been nursing her name inside him for years, even if he'd just realized it now. Immediately, he wished it'd come out differently: as if he'd spent all these years never thinking about her.

She had seemed to be deciding whether to hug him or not, but his own posture—stiff-shouldered, his body just now catching up with his bruised pride—must've warned her off, because she didn't make a move toward him.

"Davis," she said in a low tone that had always belied a prim, innocent facade. He'd always thought that Violet sounded like a Hollywood actress who hadn't found the limelight yet.

But from what he knew about the career she'd built on the city desk of the *L.A. Times,* she'd become a rising star in the world of journalism.

She stuffed her hands in her pockets, acknowledging the tension between them. "I was just walking around Old Town, taking everything in."

She glanced around the now-empty room. The silence of it echoed.

As if wanting to fill it up, she asked, "What's the occasion?"

Dancing around the past like this shouldn't bother him as much as it did. Years had gone by. He could be civil, even though he felt the anger, the shame of her leaving him creeping back up on him. "It's a fundraiser for a local charity. We had the reception in the *Recorder*'s office because the paper's been featuring different families who need some extra help these days."

She'd grown up with a lot of the hard-luck families who benefited from Helping Hand, some of them mining people who'd been struggling ever since the kaolin operation had shut down. That mine had once been the foundation of St. Valentine, producing china clay that could be used to make paper, plastic, paints and the like.

He put his champagne down on a desk. Friendly. He had to be friendly, because time had passed and he'd matured. None of it mattered now.

"So you're paying the town a visit," he said.

"I guess you could call it that." Her skin flushed as she glanced away. "It won't be for very long, though. I can't even stay *here* right now—I'm starting a shift at the Queen of Hearts."

"Helping your parents for the weekend?" God, this small talk was killing him.

Violet wandered a few steps away, robbing him of the high he felt just standing close to her. "You're going to hear this sooner or later," she said, "so I'll just tell you. I'm here temporarily because I lost my job at the *Times*. Layoffs. The economy. You know."

"I'm sorry to hear that."

He'd spent a lot of time that long-ago summer thinking bitter thoughts about her, as well as about his mother, who'd been the driving force in making Violet leave. Mom had found out that the rich kid and the miner's daughter were having a secret relationship.

Sure, he'd been the one who'd suggested keeping the meetings under the radar, "just for the summer," until college started and they could leave for L.A. together to start a new life. But, really, he had wanted secrecy because he'd been just as bad as his mom when it came to being fully aware that Violet was a miner's girl.

He bit back the memory, but echoes of the past gnawed at him.

You can do better than one of them, his mom had always said, urging him to date the cheerleaders and socialites he usually saw—all the girls who didn't do much for him except allow him to steal kisses and more.

None of them had held a candle to Violet, who was watching him now, running a slow gaze down him— from his Prada suit to the tips of his polished Justins.

His entire body beat right along with his pulse.

"Look at you. Look at all this." She laughed quietly, glancing around the small front office, with its army of computers warring with old-time pictures of the first buildings, dusty streets from the late 1920s, antique Fords and burros. The town founder, Tony Amati, sitting on the front porch of the lone hotel in what was now called Old Town, smoking a cigar down to ash.

"What's so surprising?" he asked.

"Everything. I never thought that *you* would take over the *Recorder*. I mean, you were in journalism class because it was the only elective open on the schedule senior year."

"I only wanted enough academic credits to graduate."

"But you got good at reporting, Davis."

He fought the urge to close his eyes, to let himself be that high school kid who would've allowed the sound of her speaking his name wash through him.

But he'd learned to keep his eyes wide open. Senior year, when he'd joined Violet's paper—she'd been the territorial editor—he'd only meant to slide through just another class with some smooth talk to the teacher and a minimum amount of work. But he'd found out that he was pretty good at investigating—and he'd found Violet, too.

They'd butted heads over everything—the opinionated kid from the east side of town versus the feisty girl from the west side. But he hadn't argued with her just because of his stances on the issues—he'd enjoyed seeing the fire in her eyes. It had made him feel more alive than he had ever felt before with anyone.

Then, one night, they'd stayed late, getting an edition of the *Rebel Rouser* to press.

And it'd happened.

Davis hadn't planned to kiss her. But she'd been so close to him, smelling like cherries, the warmth from her bare arms heating his skin, and he'd leaned over, feeling the hitch of her breath below his lips just before he'd pressed his mouth to hers.

Something had exploded between them that night, and up until graduation, they had met without anyone knowing about their relationship.

No one knew that they'd fallen in love.

At least, he'd thought no one had known—until his mother had confronted Violet.

He watched Violet walk toward that framed photo of Tony Amati on the wall.

"I thought for sure," she said, "that you were going to take over that mine one day."

She didn't mention it with the spite other people used in St. Valentine—the accusation reminding him of what part he'd had in the mine's shutdown. No, Davis noticed an appreciation in her expression.

Something wistful.

"Dad said you restored and reclaimed it," she added.

"That was the least I could do for the town…" He didn't finish, but it hung there in the air.

After I brought down the mine and the economy with a few newspaper stories.

He sat on the corner of his desk, watching Violet as she ran a hand over an antique Remington typewriter he'd bought on a whim, just because he could afford to.

Funny, how he was dying to let her know that he had enough to make a thousand men happy, thanks to the trust fund he'd padded with sound investments. Funny, how he wanted her to see that he'd done just fine without her after she'd left him that summer.

But that was the past speaking. Couldn't he let bygones be bygones? The damage hadn't lasted for very long. He'd forgotten her with other girls. Other women.

"Staying long?" he asked.

"Just enough time to beef up my bank account." She shrugged. "And here I thought I'd have a Pulitzer by the time I was thirty-three."

She blew out a breath, as if thinking of the dream job she'd had. Maybe she'd even lived in a condo like the sleek chrome and high-windowed place he'd had in Chicago, during his first real-life job. He'd traveled across the U.S. for a while after graduating, just to get away from his mom. Then, at the urging of Wiley Scott, who had owned the town paper, he'd gotten into Northwestern. Soon after college, he'd landed the St. Valentine kaolin mine story and returned home permanently to make up for the devastation. And he'd been doing that ever since, as if he had something to prove to the town.

Or maybe to a girl who'd seemed to believe, even for a moment, that Davis Jackson could never be more than a rich, careless playboy.

He crossed his arms over his chest. "The newspaper industry is a mess right now, so you can't take being laid off personally."

"Right," she said, obviously putting on a happy face for both of their benefits. "I know you're right."

When she looked at him again, she'd somehow managed to retrieve that confidence that had always defined Violet Osborne, a girl whose dreams had been too big for a town like St. Valentine. And to have to come back to a place she'd worked so hard to get out of…?

From the rear of the office, Davis heard the door opening, letting in the sound of laughter from the guests he was supposed to be hosting. Then it closed.

Violet heard it, too. "I should let you go."

But he didn't want that. Dammit, just seeing her again…

It brought back so much. It made him want to know if she saw the changes in him.

She offered one last, tentative smile, then moved toward the door. The sway of her hips under her pants caught Davis's eye before he forced his gaze away.

She spoke over her shoulder, hand on the doorknob. "I just wanted to congratulate you—all the things you're doing and have done for St. Valentine. All the things you've accomplished. Even my dad's been saying good things about that."

"*Your* dad complimented me?"

"I wouldn't call it complimenting, exactly. More like he was sticking up for you. He got into it with a few ex-miners once, and he pointed out that you didn't bring on that safety investigation—it was him and a few others who opened their mouths when your mother ignored their concerns after the accident."

Davis only wished that everyone in town felt the way her dad had, even if he knew the man had never liked him much, with Davis being the privileged Jackson whose family owned the mine.

And when his exposé forced a closure... Well, that left every miner but the whistleblowing ones against him. Especially the younger guys who'd been hired away by his mother to work the family's natural gas operation near Houston. It was as if they didn't realize that Davis's mom had primarily hired them on merely as an apology for what had gone down at the mine.

How anyone could've forgiven her was a mystery to Davis. After all, back when his father had owned the mine, safety had been the highest concern. His mom hadn't agreed. After his death, she'd become a big fan of money—or what she saw as security—first and foremost.

Back then, Davis had just purchased the *Recorder,* and he'd published articles about the mine based on his interviews with the whistleblowers, even though that hadn't kept one worker from nearly dying after he'd been buried in a trench while installing a drainpipe.

Then Davis had stepped up his investigation, and many folks had blamed him for the Mine Safety and Health Administration coming in. The federal organization cited inadequate procedures throughout the mine, and his mom had decided to shut down under the pressure, offering natural gas jobs out by Houston instead.

After that, the west side of St. Valentine had felt like a ghost town. And, to Davis, it'd felt doubly so with his mom. She'd accused him of writing that exposé because of a rebelliousness that had started when he'd blamed her for getting Violet to leave.

Maybe he *had* been driven by a need to show his mom that she couldn't control him, as well as a true sense of doing right for the town he'd loved enough to come back to in the end.

Violet dared to wander nearer to him, to lay a hand on his arm. The heat of her touch seared his skin.

Did she feel it?

He pulled away, cursing himself for caring.

She didn't move, and for an instant, he thought this might be the prelude to them finally saying something meaningful.

But he could see the thoughts turning in her mind. She already had everything planned out: get back on her feet with the waitressing gig, leave the town that had always looked down on her for being uppity the minute she could afford to.

The back door opened again, footsteps on the wooden planked floor...

Davis stood from the desk as Mayor Neeson and his daughter, Jennifer—a dark-haired flirt in a red dress who grinned at Davis—came into the room. She was delicately holding the stem of a champagne glass in one hand while eyeing Violet, who eyed her right back.

"Coming out for dessert anytime soon?" the mayor asked Davis, ignoring Violet altogether.

His hackles rose, just as they'd always done when he'd seen the rich kids at school dismiss Violet and her ambitions so carelessly.

Why now, though?

"Ray," Davis said, "you remember Violet Osborne?"

The mayor merely nodded to her. Jennifer instead focused on Davis as if Violet didn't even exist.

He'd had a few good times with Jennifer, and that must've given her the idea that he would be on her side. But he wouldn't let himself be that petty.

When Jennifer saw that she was alone in this, she shot a bored glance to Violet. "This is the last place I ever expected to see *you* again."

Violet didn't say a word. Instead, her shoulders stiffened.

"What brought you back?" Jennifer asked. "Did the bright, shiny world eat you up then spit you back out here?"

Davis was too busy feeling the punch of those words to notice Violet's immediate reaction.

"Jennifer…," he said.

He heard Violet mutter an "It was good to see you, Davis," just before she turned and walked out of his office, dignified, seemingly in no hurry, although he could bet she only wanted to run.

Violet felt as if she were burning up under the waning July sun as she walked as quickly as she could down the wood-planked sidewalk of Amati Street.

Mortified. Leave it to Jennifer Neeson to be the first to take a shot at her. If there was a better example of how a miner's kid with ambition didn't have a chance at breaching this town's social divides, Violet would be hard-pressed to find one.

She knew that she deserved some comeuppance for

her attitude back before she'd left town. She'd been prepared for it. That didn't mean it stung any less, though.

The dusky, heavy warmth of the afternoon took her over as she continued walking. But the prickly discomfort wasn't only coming from the weather—it had a lot to do with seeing Davis again, too.

Her body swarmed with a need she hadn't felt in such a long time—hot, rushed, breathless.

The boy who'd brought out the fun part of her... The guy who'd thought her ambitions were admirable... Davis had been everything to her at one time, and it had taken eons to push the hurt away.

Maybe it had never even left...

When she'd strolled by the newspaper office tonight, she hadn't intended to go inside. She'd been going in that direction, anyway, and the curious part of her had only wanted a peek inside the *Recorder*. Little had she known that he would be standing right there, as if waiting for her the entire time.

And when she'd seen him...

It was as if every bone in her body had turned to liquid, flowing downward, inward, swirling with so many emotions that she hadn't been able to identify them until now—disappointment at what had happened all those years ago. Surprise that Davis might just remember every bit of it. Exhilaration at seeing him again.

Back then, when Davis had first invaded her newspaper staff, she'd dismissed him. He'd worn expensive leather jackets, nice shirts—a wardrobe that probably cost what her father made in a week at the Jacksons' mine.

But Davis had intrigued her, too. And, somehow,

while they'd spent all those hours after school working on the paper, the sparring between them had turned into a few deep conversations. She'd seen beyond a rich boy into a guy who shared her intellectual curiosity about the world she longed to be a part of outside St. Valentine. She'd told him about her great-aunt Jeanne and all the stories she'd given to Violet while growing up—travels to Paris, London, cities that never slept and offered so much more opportunity than this speck of a town.

And then, when he'd first kissed her…their relationship had taken a serious turn. Until the day his mom had come to her and told her that Davis would never take any relationship seriously—especially not with a girl like Violet. That he was even seeing girls on the side right now and she shouldn't bank her future on him.

But the man Violet had seen today seemed serious enough. His shoulders were wider, his chest broader, his legs even longer than she remembered. And there was something in his gaze that was harder than it'd been before.

She reminded herself that he'd *let* her go, just as much as she'd gone. He had told her that his mom was lying about the other girls and she'd genuinely believed him, but she'd already done the damage by even asking if the words were true. It had taken merely a split second to destroy what they'd found that summer—so quickly that she'd wondered for a long time just how real their love had even been, and if they'd been much too young to know what love was.

Had all those questions only been a way of distancing herself from the anguish, though?

Right now, as her chest constricted, she wasn't sure.

The Queen of Hearts Saloon was up ahead, surrounded by the dirt road and weathered buildings. A few burros—descendants of the original silver-mining beasts of burden—lingered by the whitewashed church with its stained-glass windows. The folks up in Old Town had grown so used to them over the years that they took it upon themselves to feed them, and the tourists loved them.

She was just coming to the jewelry store when she heard hard boot steps on the boardwalk, felt a hand on her arm.

Her breath hammering from her lungs, she could only spin around and gape at Davis as he loomed over her— the jet-setting cowboy with the carefree dark blond hair and ice-blue eyes and fancy suit.

"What are you doing?" she asked, as he led her into a nearby alley, where no passersby could see them.

"I'm doing what I should've done the second you came into my office."

Here it was—the moment she had known was coming. Why had she thought she could get away with seeing him again without any consequences? All she'd wanted to do was get the awkwardness over with, knowing she was bound to run into him sometime.

"I'm here," he said, his hands planted on his hips, making him more imposing than she'd ever remembered, "to clear the air, because it sure didn't happen back there in the office."

She thought of how Mrs. Jackson, with her crisp red suit and her coiffed, bleached hair, had been waiting for Violet in the library parking lot that day, after one of her trysts with Davis in the woods out back, where it was private. They'd been so intent on keeping their relationship from their families in particular, because her dad, a miner, would've flipped, grumbling about selfish, greedy rich people and how Davis would only drop Violet when he was done with her. And Davis's mom? She was as biased as they came against "the less fortunate."

Sometimes Vi had even wondered if Davis himself liked to maintain their secret because he was afraid of public opinion, but then she'd tell herself she was crazy, that he was nothing like his mother.

Violet rested against the beaten wood wall, resigned. If he wanted to clear things up, they could do that. It was better than having to tiptoe around him for the next couple of months.

"If you want to rehash everything," she said, "we can do that."

"I never got a good answer about why you left."

All right, then. "When your mom said that this 'thing' between you and me wasn't going to last, she sounded so reasonable about it. She said that it'd be foolish to throw away my scholarship on a summer fling." Violet took a second, waiting for her runaway heartbeat to catch up, then said, "And when she said you were seeing—"

"Other girls. You know that wasn't true." Davis said it with an edge that he tamped down by gritting his jaw, looking away, as if his old anger had been rekindled, undying.

She searched for words, finally finding them. "What

do you want me to do now, Davis? What would make you feel better?"

His jaw tightened. "Nothing."

His gaze was tortured, as if there were a thousand things he wanted to say but wouldn't.

A vibration—a warmth that whirled and just about took her under—consumed her. She'd tried for so long to never be affected by what anyone in this town thought or said, but here she was, thwarted by that very thing— and it was from the man who'd affected her so acutely all those years ago.

She couldn't let down her defenses in front of him, especially now, when she needed the protection from what everyone thought or said the most.

Besides, who were they to each other anymore? She knew that he'd moved on—she'd heard stories from her mom, gossip. She'd seen the way Jennifer Neeson had glanced at him, as if they knew quite a bit about each other. He obviously hadn't shut himself away, heartbroken, because of her.

But he wanted to clear the air.

He exhaled roughly, then started to walk away, even though the air was still as thick as steam.

"You were just as confused as I was that day," she said on a choked note, stopping him. "I saw it in you. You were hurt that I was questioning you, but all I needed to hear was that you hadn't looked at another girl since we'd started seeing each other."

"I thought you already knew that."

She swallowed, her throat one big ache. "I was a kid, and your mom knew I'd be rattled by what she told me."

"You should've known that you changed everything about me, Vi."

When she glanced up, she saw more yearning in his eyes.

But then it disappeared.

He adjusted his burgundy silk tie, then started to leave again, as if they had finally knotted up their loose ends.

"I only wanted you to know that," he said.

She could barely nod.

Then after a pause in which she thought he was going to tell her—what? What could he say now?—he moved out of the alley, turning the corner, out of sight.

But not out of her heart or mind.

Chapter Two

Down the street, Violet heard laughter through the swinging doors of the Queen of Hearts, and she headed for the saloon before she made a fool of herself and went running after Davis.

They'd supposedly cleared the air, so why muddle it again?

She kept telling herself this as she walked inside the building, looking straight ahead, feeling the heavy stares of the group of elderly ladies—the knitting club—who met at the table under the rustic wagon wheel light fixture; the collection of old men at the bar who nursed mugs of beer under the whirring ceiling fans; the just-turned-twenty-one crowd who considered drinking at the Queen of Hearts in Old Town a tradition until they moved on to the newer bars in the more modern part of town.

Violet knew that she should risk a smile at them—after all, she'd be waiting on them for the first time tonight—so she tried it.

They all looked away.

Her face heated as she went to the back room, donning her old-fashioned red-and-white-striped half-apron.

"There she is!" Mom rushed up to Violet, standing on her tiptoes to give her a kiss on the cheek.

She smelled like rose perfume. Violet had always remembered that scent, even when she'd been away. It reminded her of when her mom's hair had been red, not a premature gray.

"Ready for some Friday night action?" Mom asked.

"I'm hoping for it." And so was the bank account that had dwindled during the months when she'd relied on it during a job hunt that had never borne fruit. It'd also suffered from the money she'd invested in the saloon after her parents had bought it with the last of their savings, plus all the times she'd put in more money to keep the bar and grill afloat during off-season months.

When her father came in, resplendent in the type of outfit a bartender might've worn in the late '20s, back when old Tony Amati had settled in what would become St. Valentine, she gave him a great big hug.

"Together again," he said, patting her on the back.

"I'm glad to be with you," she said.

He grinned right before he retreated to the main room's bar and her mom took over in the kitchen.

Smoothing out her apron and inhaling deeply, then exhaling, Violet followed her dad.

People were just starting to trickle in for early-bird

dinners, and as Violet took orders, everyone was civil, if not a little cool, to her.

She wished they could see just how much her time away had helped her grow out of the dreamer who'd announced her big aspirations to anyone within range— that she wasn't merely an arrogant girl who'd thought the town was beneath her.

She was several orders in when Wiley Scott, the former owner and editor of the *Recorder,* called after her.

"Why, if it isn't my favorite story chaser!" he said.

"Boisterous as ever," she said, going over to where he sat at the bar.

They hugged, and if she didn't know better, she would've thought that Wiley was putting out an extra effort to welcome her amid the other cold shoulders.

He held her away from him, giving her a paternal once-over. He was a man who looked far more likely to be at home at a chuck wagon than anywhere else. His silver hair stood up on one side, as if he'd had his hand against that part of his head as he leaned his elbow on the bar.

It was obvious that there was true pride in him as he squeezed her arm. Besides her family, he'd been one of the first people she'd told about the journalism scholarship for the University of California. Such an earned honor didn't happen to very many miner's kids in St. Valentine.

"How're you doing?" she asked.

"I hate retirement. I should've never sold the paper to Davis. That's how I'm doing."

At the sound of Davis's name, a tap-tap-tap went off

in Violet's chest. She blushed and hoped Wiley didn't notice.

"Speaking of which," he said kiddingly, "I saw you going into the *Recorder* while I was walking here. You looking for a new job?"

Obviously, her parents hadn't told him about the layoff yet.

"No." She fiddled with her ordering pad. "The *Times* had to cut staff, but something's bound to come down the pike any time now." She didn't add that she hopefully would be back on her feet and in the city long before she even had time to settle at a desk here.

"That's a real shame, but if anyone can land on all fours, it's you." He drained his beer mug. A line of foam clung to his bristled upper lip before he wiped it away with his flannel shirtsleeve. "Too bad you won't stick around for a place on the *Recorder,* though. You and Davis made a good team back in the day. I remember how well you two worked together whenever you'd come in to get the school paper printed in the office."

She thought of standing next to Davis just under a half hour ago, thought of how good he still smelled, like cedar chips, fresh and manly.

Manly. He was a *man,* no longer a boy, and her body was reacting to that.

She realized it'd been like that, too, back in high school, every time he'd stood close by, leaning over her shoulder while she'd typed up a story.

And she would've pretended to ignore him before he'd broken open her emotional dam with one kiss. But, deep down, she would've gone weak, her pulse warbling as she wished he would tease her some more. That he would adore her just as much as she did him, even though she would've died before admitting it first.

Not that any of it mattered now, even as Wiley gave her a mischievous glance, as if he could tell just what she was thinking.

Obviously, when he'd retired from reporting, he hadn't left everything behind.

Violet signaled to her dad behind the bar so he'd get Wiley another beer. "Anything else you need?"

He rested a hand on her arm. "Yeah. I need for you to keep that chin up, even as you're eating humble pie."

He didn't have to explain—not when he was sending a loaded look to the rest of the people in the room.

Like her great-aunt Jeanne, Wiley had pumped up all her aspirations. It was just that he hadn't died and left her with the final advice of *Follow your dreams for me, okay?* That push had persuaded Violet that she needed to leave this little town and go for it outside someday.

She half smiled at his suggestion. Humble pie. Sounded appropriate for a person who'd returned here temporarily to lick her wounds. But how could she take that first step with everyone, show them that she didn't hold St. Valentine in contempt as much as they probably thought she did?

Before she could ask Wiley, his gaze widened as he looked at something behind her.

When she turned around, she almost smacked into the wall of a man's chest.

She looked up into Davis Jackson's face, his blue eyes unreadable, and her blood began to churn in her veins.

She couldn't do much more than stare up at Davis, who had loosened the tie from around his neck, giving him a devil-may-care appearance. He'd shocked her with his unexpected presence, and now desire was flaring over her, sending the fine hairs on her arms to standing straight.

She didn't have to guess what he was seeing in her—her eyes were probably like a fawn in the headlights. And the heat on her cheeks…

Probably couldn't be more obvious.

As they locked gazes, someone turned on the juke-box, and a Carrie Underwood song brought Violet back to earth.

"Your party's over?" she asked over the tune as Davis stood by a bar stool next to Wiley.

"I skipped dessert but said my good-nights and closed up the office. The mayor is kindly handling the stragglers in the tents out back." He glanced around, and a redhead Violet didn't know gave Davis a look that just about shouted out that he knew her. As in maybe even biblically.

"The night's still young enough here," he said, loosening his tie even more as he nodded to the woman. She raised an eyebrow at him then went back to the man she'd been talking to.

Violet was confused. Why had Davis even come to the saloon when he should've been avoiding her?

Maybe he was just bent on making some kind of point to her—that he could move on with a social life, and certainly already *had*.

That had always been his reputation with the girls.

But Vi had discovered there was much more to him—a soul filled with longings about the world outside, a boy who missed the father who'd died when he was only four years old.

He was a person who was capable of finding someone to love, even if he seemed to be the last guy who'd ever fall into it....

Wiley got up from his seat, saying something about a trip to the john. Davis hovered, staring down at Vi, even as she tried to avoid his gaze.

She felt it, though, as if he were the only other person in the room. The weight of that stare thrilled her through and through.

"Davis," she whispered. A warning, slightly panicked because of what he was doing to her—what she couldn't afford during this temporary detour in her life.

When she finally risked a glance at him, he had that look again—the same fervent one he'd worn after he'd first kissed her all those years ago.

Then it disappeared, as if it'd never happened.

"Whiskey," Davis said to her, sitting on the stool next to Wiley's.

He doffed his jacket, leaving her with a view of muscle underneath linen, the hint of tanned skin at his neck.

She tried not to look, even though it was hard not to.

She left him so she could place his order and take care of her other tables, but the entire time she knew he was there, at the bar, watching.

Just as she was about to scream from the tension, her sixth sense tickled her, and she turned around to see a man walking through the swinging doors of the entrance and toward the other end of the bar, near a corner where liquor bottles caught the light.

Another customer in her section, thank God. More reason to keep busy.

To keep away from Davis.

The new guy was wearing a black cowboy hat low over his brow, and he didn't take it off, even as he slouched onto the stool. He used one hand to pick up a laminated menu and laid the other flat on the wood in front of him, almost as if they'd all gone back in time and he was ready to draw for a gunfight.

But it was only when he tipped back his hat that the room went silent.

"The spitting image," a customer muttered to his dining partner.

Violet didn't have to ask what he was talking about— not when she had such clear sight of the thick dark hair over the man's brow, the coal-black eyes, the rough-and-tumble hardness of a face that she and all the other town folk had seen in many an old picture.

She turned her gaze to the nearby wall, where a grainy photograph of their town founder, Tony Amati, hung.

Thick dark hair, coal-black eyes. Same jaw. Same toughness.

The spitting image, all right. It was downright eerie.

From the way everyone was staring, she could tell that nobody had ever seen this guy before. Who *was* he?

Her curiosity sharpened, she nonetheless stopped by table three to deliver beverages first, then detoured to table four for their order, running it to her mom, who was cooking at the grill. Then she returned to the stranger's corner, trying to act as if the entire room wasn't fascinated by him.

"Hi," she said, putting on the smiles. "Welcome to the Queen of Hearts."

"Thanks." When the man looked up at her, his gaze was dark. Uneasy.

It struck Violet that he knew very well that he was the center of attention. That maybe he had even come in here to accomplish just that.

"Do you need some time to look at the menu?" she asked, pen poised over paper.

"I'll start with a beer. Bottled." His voice was raspy, reminding her of a scratched record that someone had unearthed from storage. "Then we'll go with a buffalo burger, rare."

"Great."

He glanced around the room, slowly. Deliberately. "Do all tourists get this much interest from the locals?"

"Not really." She glanced toward the back of the room, taking care to avoid focusing on Davis, who had his back to her, although she was sure that he was just as aware of her as she was of him.

She fixed her gaze on a photo of Tony Amati hanging near the jukebox. "It's just that you look like…"

"Who?" he asked casually.

"Tony Amati, our town founder. He goes way back in the history books here." She cocked her head. "You could be his twin."

The stranger glanced toward the photo.

"Want to see it up close?" she asked.

He shrugged. "Why not?"

Before she fetched it, she went to the kitchen, handing off her ticket. When she walked out to the bar, Wiley had returned to his seat, hunched over his beer, not saying a word.

Davis caught her by the apron. She stifled a gasp; his hand was near her hip, and the patch of skin under her pants burned with his imprint.

"Who's that guy?" he asked.

"Don't know." She tugged away from him, making it *her* point to show him that touching her wasn't allowed, even if they had "cleared the air."

Her skin was still humming when she left. And to make matters worse, the sensation was spreading along her hip, getting to places that Davis Jackson had no right getting to.

After she fetched the photo from the wall, she got back to the stranger's table. He seemed to drink in the picture, but she couldn't get any more than that out of him.

"Tony Amati never had kids, so you couldn't be a direct descendant," she said. "Then again, don't they say everyone in the world has a doppelgänger?"

The stranger narrowed his eyes at the photo. "I suppose we bear a resemblance to each other."

In spite of all the reading she loved to do, as well as the Founder's Weekend celebrations, which seemed to honor the town and not the man, Tony had always remained somewhat of a mystery, no matter how much digging she'd done. Evidently, he'd been a private sort who'd never talked about where he'd come from, one who'd re-invented himself out west, as so many others had done. He'd been rumored to be a Texas Ranger and had been wealthy, helping out families in the area. And then there was the matter of his death…the biggest mystery about Tony Amati.

The stranger kept his gaze on the photograph a little longer before handing it back to her. She tried to read him again, but he was like stone, his face etched into a hard-bitten expression that revealed nothing.

She also felt that familiar thrill of a mystery—answers to be chased and caught. She almost even felt just as she used to when she'd gone to her real job every day.

"As interesting as all this is," he said, "I'm really just passing through this place."

"Well, it's good to have you around for however long you're here…"

"Jared," he said, offering no more than that.

"I'm Violet, and I'll be right back with your beer."

But after she fetched it from the bar, Jared proved very untalkative, settling into his seat, pulling his hat back down over his brow, ignoring the remainder of the stares from the rest of the patrons.

Davis had left the Queen of Hearts long before last call, but that didn't mean he'd gone home to his ranch on the outskirts of town. He was restless. His mind, his body…neither of them could shut down.

Not with Violet here again.

He'd gone back to the newspaper office, firing up his computer, intending to get some work done. But he kept seeing Violet with her apron around the hips he'd once stroked with his hands, kept seeing her making her way around the bar and grill tonight, chancing smiles at anyone who wasn't him.

Hell, she'd even seemed more comfortable with that stranger who'd wandered into the saloon.

Davis forced his mind to focus on the Tony Amati look-alike. An idea had sparked in him, in spite of his ridiculous fascination with Violet, and he tried to put all his energies into the distraction now.

Anything to take his mind off her. *Anything.*

A story about a look-alike such as this stranger would be a hell of an angle for Founder's Weekend, he thought. *The past arises in St. Valentine...*

He tried to forget just how personally relevant that thought was as he did a computer search that turned up next to nothing about Tony Amati. Afterward, Davis accessed the digitized archives and skimmed through old editions of the *Recorder,* just to see if there was anything to keep him even busier.

He didn't know a whole lot of personal stuff about the town founder, and, from the looks of it, there was a whole lot less than Davis had expected to discover about a man who'd been so key to this town's development.

But, after about an hour of frustration, he finally did uncover something. A tidbit that would require much more research.

An article with the headline: Amati Dies of Unknown Causes.

The text was extremely vague, just an extended obituary about Amati's love of privacy and his leadership qualities. It was as if Tony's death hadn't rocked St. Valentine much at all. Then again, common knowledge had always maintained that he'd died alone, out of the public eye.

When Davis saw another article, planted deep in the back of the same edition, he looked even closer.

Sheriff Kills Burglars in Home.

Davis went over that story, too, yet it offered about as much as Amati's obituary had.

He didn't know what it was exactly, but something was poking at him—the "other" sense all reporters relied on.

That nudge-nudge that kept them up at nights.

There wasn't much else to go on, but it was a mystery Davis decided to pursue in his spare time, between overseeing the next biweekly edition and reporting on preparations for Founder's Weekend so the story could go out to bigger outlets, hopefully attracting some visitors to St. Valentine in a week.

It'd be just what this town needed…and what he needed for them.

He locked up the office at midnight, spying Mr. and Mrs. Osborne and Violet coming out of the bar and grill down the street.

Was it his imagination when he saw Violet hesitate as they secured the big doors in front of the saloon's entrance? Was she looking toward the newspaper office because her reporter radar was up and running, too, after meeting the stranger?

Or was she looking down here for a different reason altogether, one that made Davis's reluctant heartbeat race? Was she just as eager to see him once again as he was her?

As Davis caught Violet's gaze under the moonlight, he couldn't move. He was frozen by the hunger for her that had only grown hour by hour, sending him to the Queen of Hearts after his party, even after he'd made it crystal clear that he'd found closure with her.

But had he?

Violet seemed to be under the same spell, unmoving, as her parents headed toward their truck, which was parked in an alley beside the building.

Davis couldn't stay away, and he moved toward Violet. Standing near their vehicle, her father watched Davis from beneath the brim of his cowboy hat.

"Gary," Davis said, nodding to him, then greeted his wife, as well.

Andrea Osborne smiled at Davis but her husband merely grunted out Davis's name. Despite their having worked together to shut down the mine, there was still an avalanche of disappointment there—a father's hard feelings for the kid who'd broken his daughter's heart once upon a time.

Davis came to a stand in front of Violet, who was still near the bar's doorway. His blood sang through him— all he wanted to do was touch her, just as free and easy as they had been in high school.

"Saw you talking to that stranger," Davis said, straight to the point. "Did you find out who he is?"

"His name is Jared."

"And?"

"And what? He wanted something to eat and he's probably miles out of town by now."

Davis had the feeling that she meant to end the conversation right there with him, but he wouldn't let that happen. And, truthfully, it wasn't just because he wanted this story.

What the hell *did* he want, though?

"I already did a little research," he said.

"You did?" she asked.

There was a spark in her—the reporter's excitement that had turned him on back when they'd worked on the school paper.

"You do know," he said, "that I do a lot of the reporting around here." His trust fund investments gave him that luxury in sleepy St. Valentine.

Before she could respond, her dad said, "Violet?"

He apparently wanted to scoot back to their ranch, where Violet was no doubt staying.

"They're my ride," she said. "I came home to find my old car dead in the barn. It's being fixed."

"If you want a look at the archives to see what you can find out about Amati," Davis said, "you could stick around. I could drive you home, since your family's place is on the way to my own."

Had he really just said that?

Even under the gas lamps that lined the street, he could see how Violet's gaze had gone wide. Her eyes were like brandy—something he could get drunk on.

But then she looked toward her waiting parents, and Davis could just about guess what was going through her mind.

She hadn't come back to St. Valentine to mess around with an old flame—she was here to recover and regroup. And the minute she got the chance to skedaddle out of town again, she wouldn't have time for Podunk stories like this one.

"I'm opening the saloon with Mom in the morning," she said, an excuse if he'd ever heard one.

But he could still detect the temptation in her tone. The story had intrigued her.

As he heard her parents' truck doors slam shut, temptation swarmed him. An opportunity—a lure for Violet to come around his office, for him to see her again.

Bad idea, said a little voice inside him. *Real bad.*

Nonetheless, he heard himself saying, "Did you know that the paper didn't report on Amati's cause of death? He's a presence in those saloon photographs and in town history, so why was he practically a nobody in his obituary?"

"You'll get to the bottom of it."

The same anger that had haunted him for years reared up again. He wasn't going to let her get away that easily this time. "Something's going on here. And if it's big enough, it might even serve to bring in some much-needed tourists to St. Valentine. It could pump up the economy, and that includes the saloon, Vi."

She blew out a breath, as if he'd hit a mark.

It wasn't fair, but he said it anyway. "This story could really give this town some profile. And working on it might also go a long way in making your stay here easier."

"Why would you say that?"

"I've seen what you're going through—the looks, the snide remarks."

"Jennifer was the only one offering up the sarcasm."

"We both know she won't be the last."

As she took that in, he waited. *Say yes, Vi...*

"Do you really think this look-alike will amount to anything?" she asked.

"Yeah. Just call it a gut feeling."

Another hesitation. She was going to tell him to stick this story where the sun didn't shine, wasn't she? The worst thing about it was that he knew another no from her would chew at him for the rest of the night, the rest of...

He wasn't sure just how long it'd be.

"Davis," she said softly, "I can guess how much it would mean for you if you could do something wonderful for this place."

"Earlier, I swear I saw the girl who never turned her back on a story. Where did she go?"

"You know where she went."

A short burst from her parents' pickup horn made her walk away. But he still felt her on his flesh, singeing away at him.

"Violet?" he asked.

She stopped in her tracks.

His pulse was flying. "The newspaper office will be open tomorrow before you get to the saloon."

She bit her bottom lip, glancing at the bar and grill.

He pushed the subject, his heartbeat racing. "I'll be passing your ranch on the way in." Damned if he wasn't going to give up. Damned if he was going out on a limb here, against all his common sense.

Her parents' truck purred as she gave him that wide-eyed look that told him the promise of making a gesture of goodwill to the town mattered to her just as much as it did to him.

"Okay," she said. "I can look at the archives for about an hour, just to see if there's anything to this."

"And to do a freelance write-up for the *Recorder?*"

"If the research pans out. Maybe."

Was she about to say something more?

He never found out, because she'd already jumped into her parents' truck, leaving Davis with a tight grin.

He'd lost her once, but he had her for a morning now.

Chapter Three

After a night of searching the internet on her laptop without much success, Violet was up just after dawn, the birds chirping outside the window of the little cabin she was staying in on her parents' ranch.

Back in the days before her mother and father had purchased the saloon, when Dad was a full-timer at the mine, Mom and the Osbornes' employees had run this spread that had been in the family for generations. They'd bred American Quarter horses until, after several bad years of business, they'd had to sell off most of the land and stop the operation altogether. That was when her parents had decided to invest everything they had left in the bar and grill, and this decision had left the employee cabins empty, except for this one. Mom had fixed it up just before Violet had arrived, trimming it with gingham curtains and polishing the pine furniture. It was a stark contrast to her old apartment, with its view of Wilshire Boulevard's skyscrapers in the near distance and the elevator just down the hall, where every doorway seemed to hide an actor or a budding director behind it.

She left the cabin, knowing Mom would've cooked an amazing breakfast—chocolate chip pancakes. It'd been a while since Violet had eaten such a thing; not since her last short trip here months ago. Her job had kept her too busy to be in the kitchen very much, and she'd become accustomed to grabbing hot coffee and limp sandwiches on the fly.

She opened the main house's front door, the aroma of those pancakes making her mouth water. From the entryway, she could see the hall leading to the bedrooms—the one she'd grown up in would still be untouched, with its posters of all the places Great-Aunt Jeanne had experienced while writing her upscale magazine travel articles—Monaco, Madrid, Berlin. Whenever Great-Aunt Jeanne had visited, she'd always told Violet about salon talks with poets, riding in speedboats with princes.

She would've been proud that Violet had spread her wings and explored everything outside this "hick town" that she had escaped, too.

Violet just tried not to dwell on what her aunt would've done if she knew her great-niece had landed back in St. Valentine.

She made her way into the kitchen, the whoosh from an overhead fan chasing away some of the heat already settling in for the day.

Mom was wielding a spatula at the stove, her curly

gray hair in a ponytail. "Just a few more minutes and I'll be done."

"Can't wait."

"We can have a family breakfast, just like we used to. Your dad's going to be out of the shower anytime now."

Oops. On the way home last night, Violet had neglected to tell her parents that Davis would be picking her up this morning. Mom would be okay with it, but Dad?

He emerged earlier than expected from the hallway, his graying head wet from the shower. "It'll be a scorching one today." He bent down to kiss the top of Violet's head and sat for their family meal.

Might as well get this over with. "I wish I could stick around for a long breakfast this morning," she said, "but I'm off to town soon."

Mom looked over her shoulder, balancing a pancake on the spatula. "How are you going to get there?"

"It's covered." Violet nonchalantly poured herself a glass of orange juice from the pitcher on the table. "Davis is picking me up."

Dad sat up straighter in his chair, so Violet spoke before he could.

"I'm working on a small story that could bring some positive attention to St. Valentine in time for Founder's Weekend."

"Hmph," Dad said.

"Gary," Mom said. "Don't start."

Violet said, "There's really nothing to start about. It's work, and I can add it to my résumé so future bosses can see that I'm still sharpening my craft."

She neglected to add that she'd been happy when Davis hadn't brought up anything personal again last night, after he'd caught her post-closing time at the bar and grill. When he'd started talking about the stranger instead, she'd just about wilted with relief. Yeah, that's what it had to be—relief. Because surely it hadn't been some kind of disappointment that they were veering around everything else in favor of talking about the Tony Amati look-alike.

Mom brought the platter of pancakes to the table, but Dad didn't dig in just yet.

"That's all it is?" Dad asked. "A story?"

"Yes. I figure it might…I don't know, it might go a long way in showing everyone that I want to contribute while I'm around. Coming back here made me realize that I have some things to clean up in this town."

Mom sat down, too. "And a news story's going to do that?"

"It could. It's a gesture, a way of saying that I'm not any better than anyone here. That I do care about this place." Violet picked up her orange juice glass.

"So," Mom said, "does that mean you're going to stay longer than we first thought?"

Violet laughed. "Adventure's in my blood, Mom, just like it was with Great-Aunt Jeanne. I miss running around the city, writing about the different trials at court or about what's being smuggled in through LAX. I miss meeting my friends for cocktails and going to movies at the Chinese Theatre—"

Mom held up a hand. "I don't want to hear about

smugglers and criminals." She liked to pretend that Violet had a nice, cushy desk job.

Dad stabbed at a pancake on the platter. "I'm about as excited about you working with Davis as I was when you were kids."

"Gary…" Mom said again, this time with more warning.

Dad knitted his bushy brows as Mom continued.

"Violet's an adult. Just because she's living here doesn't mean we get to poke our nose into her business." She spread a checkered napkin over her lap. "Besides, you'd think we've grown out of all this—who's rich, who's poor, especially after Davis went to bat for the miners."

"Too bad it backfired," Violet said.

Dad stuffed a bite of pancake into his mouth.

Violet didn't let him off the hook. "He deserves points for what he's doing for St. Valentine now, too, Dad. He's determined to get this place on its feet again."

Mom shot Dad a "You hear that?" look.

Violet polished off one pancake, knowing she could take some with her, plus her juice, then rose from the table just before her dad did. Dad said he needed to do some saloon paperwork before going in for the day.

She rushed to brush her teeth in her cabin. When she got back into the main house, the sound of a deep, low male voice came from the kitchen. That zinging sensation flew through Violet again.

Davis.

She took a big breath. *Steady. You're just helping him with some research.*

But when she saw him standing in the kitchen near the stove—talking with her mom, dressed in a tailored Western shirt, jeans and expensive handworked leather boots—her heart just about leaped out of her chest.

Her mind scrambled, right along with all the crazy electricity flying through her body, and she wasn't so sure today was about being professional at all.

They'd taken some pancakes with them, driving the country road in Davis's shiny, vintage Aston Martin.

Out of the corner of his eye, he watched Violet nibble on a pancake. He'd never been so interested in the way a woman ate. He'd never even dwelled so much on a mouth and what it might feel like against his own. And this was a very adult craving, too—far from the hormonal interest he'd had in Violet way back when.

He rested one arm on the open window, welcoming the morning air as it hit his face. It didn't do much to cool him off, though.

Davis had just finished telling Violet more of the details he'd culled from his research last night when she brushed a few pancake crumbs from her blouse.

"I think that a break-in at the sheriff's home the same week that Tony died under mysterious circumstances is worth looking into," she said, all business. "I don't know, it could be my imagination getting spooked, but—"

"We could have some kind of a lead about how Tony Amati really might've died?"

"Could be."

"I even wonder if our stranger, Jared, has come here

to find out about Tony, too. If he's his descendent or something and he's on a fact-finding trip."

Violet turned toward him, and Davis glanced at her. A few dark red hairs had escaped from her ponytail. Her brown eyes had a gleam—that unmistakable sign of the thrill of the chase that used to light her gaze in their high school days.

Outside the window, white fences and green pastures rushed by. "You're enjoying this, aren't you?" she asked.

"What—this story, or having you in my car, riding along with me?"

She blushed, and it stirred him right back up again. It also warned him that he needed to back off, because it probably wouldn't take much for her to shy away from him.

"It has nothing to do with your four-wheeled toys." Now Violet had that lost expression on her face he'd seen so many times before. "I meant to say that you seem to like the possibility of chasing a real story. More than the usual 'Fireman Rescues Cat from Tree' sort of thing."

"We get a little more action than that in St. Valentine these days. Last month, we actually covered a knock-down-drag-out fight between Maura Stosser and our own Wiley Scott. She'd bopped him on the head in the general store with an umbrella from the sale rack when he'd given her the wrong look."

"What look was that?"

"Cross-eyed. I don't know. Wiley and Maura fight like a dog and cat. He's always straddled the line between the miners and the townies, but Maura's a..."

He wasn't sure how to put it without offending Violet.

"Devoted east-side girl who doesn't think anyone should straddle?" she supplied, laughing, letting him know that she didn't live by all the labels. She never had.

"Really," she said, getting back to the previous topic, "you don't mind the slow pace of this town?"

He steered onto Ranger Street, which bypassed the newer part of town and led to the old section. "Believe it or not, I'm perfectly content here. Even when I took a break from St. Valentine after high school, I never did get comfortable with skyscrapers and concrete. I like the open blue. I like the sound of silence in the morning just after the sun rises. I'm merely simple at heart, I guess."

"You're not simple at all."

She said it as if he'd *never* been that way.

Would he have been enough to keep her interested? He didn't know what the hell he'd do with an answer, but not knowing was eating away at him. He'd spent a lot of time finding himself after she'd left.

Why did it seem so damned important for her to acknowledge that he would've never disappointed her?

He pulled the car into a spot behind the newspaper office in a plume of dust. As the cloud hovered, they closed up the windows, then alighted, going inside through the back entrance, past the printing equipment and into the main room.

After he snapped on the light, Violet put her hands on her hips and glanced around. She was wearing a crisp white blouse, creased dark blue shorts and Keds, and Davis took a moment to appreciate how her legs seemed to go on forever.

Finally, she said, "Every modern convenience known

to man, even air-conditioning. This doesn't feel like the same place Wiley owned."

He pulled out a padded leather chair so she could commandeer a computer. She sat right down as he turned on the unit.

He brought her some bottled water from the office fridge and sat at a neighboring computer station to search the digitized archives for other relevant past editions. Every once in a while, though, he couldn't help glancing at her. He liked how she bit her bottom lip when she was concentrating, liked how she tilted her head, as if that helped her thought process, too.

Something in his chest got all warm. She was serious; he wasn't all that much. She was a mining kid; he was a Jackson.

But would that matter so much anymore?

"Look at this," Violet said.

She was pointing to her screen, and he leaned in to her, looking over her shoulder.

His cheek was only an inch away from her hair, and he could feel the light brush of it, plus the warmth from her skin. He could smell more subtleties in the lotion or shampoo she used—cherry laced with...almond. Something that burrowed deep into him.

It took him a second to gather his wits, but he eventually forced himself to read the article she'd indicated.

It was dated a day after those other articles he'd found about the break-in at the sheriff's house and Tony's death.

"Sheriff Hadenfield's daughter, Tessa..." he said, skimming. "...Hospital...resting comfortably..."

He backed away before he could do something foolish, like bend down and press his mouth to Violet's. "This is about as vague as the rest of what we have."

"Isn't that weird? I've been reading other articles from this era and they're not as haphazardly researched and reported."

"I hate to say the word *conspiracy,* but it's flashing in my mind like neon."

They kept looking at each other for a second, then broke into tentative smiles that disappeared all too soon.

"Right," he said. "Some kind of conspiracy here in little St. Valentine. Now that would be something to capitalize on. A great legend that outside news stations could report on, making us a countrywide vacation destination, just like Tombstone or Dodge City."

But Violet was already tilting her head. "Davis, what if the sheriff had enough power to keep whatever happened under wraps?"

"Why would he want to do that?"

"I'm not sure. And there are no Hadenfields left in St. Valentine to enlighten us."

But she was already out of her chair, the wheels turning, and he couldn't help feeling the same excitement that was setting her in motion.

"Do you think the new hospital would have Tessa's records either in hard copy or online?" Violet asked. "Unless some kind of privacy laws stopped us, could we find out what sort of injuries she had?"

"When the old hospital burned down in '63, all the paper went with it. They wouldn't have had the chance to digitize their files." In spite of this setback, he grinned at her. Whether she'd admit it or not, she *was* working with him again.

She rolled her eyes. "So I'm a little invested already."

Then, with a soft smile, she went back to her computer, printing out the article. He didn't ask her when she'd like to show up to work with him next. He wished he could just offer her a salary, put her on staff full-time, but he expected that would only make her bristle. Getting her to consider doing something freelance had been tough enough.

Just why did she have to be so...*Violet*? So hard to negotiate with? Then again, if she weren't so complicated, he would've never been interested.

When he caught her running her fingers over the printout while rereading it, his skin reacted, just as if she was brushing over him. His belly clenched.

Was it wrong that he was thinking of what it would be like if she touched him with the same dedication she was showing to a career? What would it be like to have that kind of devotion?

He cleared away the thoughts, went back to work. They both kept at it, too, until she glanced at her wrist-watch then stretched her arms over her head. He tried not to look—really he did—but as her shirt pressed against her breasts, he couldn't stop himself.

Hot summer nights...a picnic blanket spread out beneath the old oak near Jenner's Field...his mouth on hers, his hands...

Once again, the words were out of his mouth before he could second-guess the wisdom of saying them.

"Married to a career," he muttered.

She crossed her arms over her chest, as if realizing only now that she'd let her guard down around him. "What?"

"I said, 'Married to a career.' I thought you'd go to the city, find whatever it was you were looking for there, maybe even a better boyfriend, then live happily ever after with him. But maybe you were just too independent for that. You always were."

Her jaw had tensed, and she got busy on the computer again.

He leaned back in his chair. "I won't ask you about how life treated you these past years. We'll avoid all that and have a great working relationship instead."

"I like that idea."

"Wasn't there anyone?" He couldn't help it. Curiosity—jealousy?—was getting the better of him.

She stopped moving her mouse around. "All right, I'll humor you just this once. I do date. But I'm very busy, rushing around on the job and all that. At least, I was."

His heart flinched in his chest, then just waited there, seeing if she'd open up any more than this.

Blushing, she seemed to lose the ability to speak, and he wanted to tell her that she should look at him—really look and see that she'd made a bad choice fifteen summers ago.

He almost laughed at that. Him, the man with a mansion on his ranch property, the man who threw parties where the guests drank Cristal, and *this* was all he wanted. One more stolen moment with her.

She glanced at her watch again. "Would it be okay if I came back later?"

She wanted to come *back*? "Sure. Jason Edgett puts the editions to bed these days, so he'll be coming in soon. That'll give me a chance to do more digging. I'll let you know if I find anything." His devilish streak was still going strong. "We could meet at the diner for a briefing after you get off your waitressing shift."

She pressed her lips together, as if ready to call him out on crossing the professional line they'd agreed on.

Then, the old Violet returned—saucy, always giving as good as she got from him. "Seven o'clock?"

"Seven it is."

After she left, he kept looking at the door, wondering just how safe she would feel if she knew that his attraction was alive and well whenever he was around her.

What was she doing?

As Violet stood outside the Orbit Diner, its silver siding just as shiny in the dusk as it'd been when she'd last eaten there in high school, she hesitated to go inside.

She shouldn't be having dinner with Davis.

But she was. Her pulse was darn well skipping along, as a matter of fact, and it'd be doing the same all day, as she'd waited tables and tried not to think about him.

And that was a bad thing, too. When she worked a story, that was where her mind usually was—eating, sleeping, living the facts and questions, and trying to weave them all together.

Yet now?

Now she would find herself thinking of *him*—of that perennially tousled dark blond hair. Of those blue eyes that could talk a girl into almost anything.

Even a girl like her, who didn't stop for distractions.

But Violet had overcome distractions before. That was how she'd succeeded, by driving in a straight line, full speed ahead, through roadblocks and over speed bumps.

She would do it this time, too. There was even a chance that if there was a big story hidden somewhere under the dirt of St. Valentine, it might go a long way in not only ingratiating her to the town but landing her a new job at another solid paper, as well.

Feeling more positive now, she went into the diner, looking around at the aqua-upholstered booths, the shiny chrome-and-Formica decor. It seemed like a figment of her imagination, nearly washed away by her time in the city—lunch hours spent at a cluttered desk, happy hours at upscale hot spots where she could see the traffic jams outside the window. But the diner was well-worn, and hardly cosmopolitan; it had reminded her of what someone from the 1950s would've predicted the future might look like with plastic bubbles curved over the pie selections, and the spaceship fins winging off the main counter.

She finally found Davis in a rear booth, a menu in front of his face. As she went to him, she walked past the suddenly silent old-timers who sat around all day drinking coffee and gossiping. By the counter, two of them even had a chess game going. She wasn't sure, but she thought it might've been a game that had lasted since she was in high school, with the same bearded players.

They were so involved with their playing and socializing that they offered only civil nods along with lingering, maybe even resentful, looks. It was a start, she supposed.

By the time she reached Davis, he still had his menu up.

She cleared her throat, and when he lowered the menu, revealing that breathtaking, chiseled face of his, she knew he'd just been testing her again, ignoring her until the last instant.

Her heart blipped, but she quieted it. All business between them, right?

She got the briefing started as she sat down. "Any progress?"

"Not on my watch."

Damn.

"Okay, then," she said. "All that means is that we start interviewing now. We've got plenty of resources in this town." She gestured around the diner. "I'll bet half these people were around when Tony was, even if they were just kids. They might remember something that'll give us another lead."

"Plenty of resources, all right." He gave her a look that said he noted how she was willing to talk to everyone when they might not give her the time of day.

She'd talked to much tougher people than the ones in St. Valentine, though—alleged criminals, their lawyers. No one scared her.

Leaving Davis out of *that* equation, she glanced at the menu, pretty much already knowing what she wanted. There were a lot of things she'd thought were small-time about St. Valentine, but one of them wasn't the Orbit's patty melt. No one else out in the world seemed to know how to cook one like they did.

The waitress stopped by to take their orders, and afterward, Violet got out an iPad from her purse.

"Maybe," she said, turning it on, "we should throw around some names and organize a plan of attack. It'd be a waste of time if we both tried to interview the same people."

He leaned back in the booth, his arms resting on the top of the seat. The fine linen of his shirt outlined the muscles in his arms, probably honed from ranch work since she'd heard that he liked to let off steam on his small spread.

Again, she was trying diligently to not gape at those muscles, but she couldn't help imagining how his arms would feel wrapped around her. How they had felt long ago.

Not knowing how else to act around him, she accessed the notebook function in her iPad, as restless as usual.

He chuckled quietly, with that edge that always seemed to accompany anything he said. "You can't wait to hightail it out of here as soon as you can."

"The diner or town?"

"Both, I'd say." He glanced around. "You know, that stings, Vi. I bought this place a few years ago. I can't imagine anyone wanting to leave it."

He'd bought a lot of property—his ranch outside the town limits, the paper, more than a few tourist-related shops, not to mention other acreage he still hadn't developed.

"I like the diner," she said mildly. "I always have."

"Then why are you on pins and needles?"

Oh, he was really goading her, wasn't he? And she had the feeling that he was working on an entirely different level of conversation than it first seemed—talking about leaving in general.

Talking about her betrayal so long ago.

"I'm just naturally high-strung," she said, not taking his bait.

"So it has nothing to do with—"

"Listen, as much as you want to hear me say I regret what happened, I like the life I made for myself out in the world."

The look on his face stopped her tirade. She wasn't sure what it was, but it struck her as...

No, he couldn't still be heartbroken. She'd even convinced herself years ago that he never *had* been, since he'd always been so cool to her whenever she'd call him from her dorm, trying to make amends. Until she'd given up altogether.

Maybe it'd be okay for her to capitulate a little right now, with him looking this way. Maybe it'd be okay for her to say something that had nothing to do with business for once.

"The last few years made me who I am now," she said softly. "I have good friends who threw me a party when I had to leave. I had an apartment across from the Farmer's Market near the Grove, where all the movie stars hang out, and we'd go there to spot celebrities and see what they wore and how they handled the paparazzi.

I had my dream job, and I found out that I could do it pretty damn well, too. I learned so much about myself."

A pang invaded her. After being laid off, she wasn't so confident about doing well anywhere, but she tried not to let that show.

Yet Davis had always had her number when no one else did, and now he leaned forward, resting his arms on the table, his startlingly blue eyes searching her gaze.

"With all of that did you ever think of what might've happened if you hadn't gone, Vi?"

Her heart smarted as she felt herself being pulled back to the past.

And, scariest of all, back to him.

Chapter Four

If she hadn't gone...

The comment reverberated through Davis. He had imagined what life with Violet might've been like a million times, but even more forcefully, the fantasies of what they *had* had with each other flooded him now....

Two kids who were riding in his hot rod past county lines, until they arrived at a private place he'd discovered one recent day—a grove of trees under the summer night sky, the stars peeking through the branches, a few blankets in the backseat, his hands actually trembling as he cut the engine then turned to her.

"So," she said, her red hair longer back then, down past her shoulders, tied back by a blue ribbon. He'd remembered the blue a long time afterward, remembered so many colors and sensations.

Her cheeks were flushed, and she ran her palms down

her prim skirt, as if she were just as nervous and suddenly awkward as he was.

"So," he echoed.

She leaned forward, turned on the radio, and the inside of his car filled with the murmur of an old, slow country tune. Johnny Lee, gentle and hopeful.

Tonight, for the first time since he'd started dating, Davis wasn't sure how to handle a girl. A woman—because that's what Violet was to him. With her, he was someone who wanted to explore the world by her side, someone with curiosity about life and more drive than he could've ever imagined.

Right now, under the moonlight, he was too overcome to even kiss her.

Smiling at him shyly, she slipped her hand behind his head, pulling him down until their lips were flush, crushing, seeking. His universe spun, throwing him in a thousand directions.

They came up for breath and he cupped her face in one hand, looking into her brown eyes.

The universe was in her gaze, the future.

"Are you sure?" he asked.

"I've never been surer about anything."

His pulse was wild, nearly tearing him apart while he reached back, untying the ribbon in her hair.

Her locks spread over her shoulders, and he buried his face in them, then in her neck, making her gasp as he pressed tiny kisses against her skin, against the throb of a vein.

Each beat spelled out the promises they had already made to each other—vows that would go beyond the summer. Vows that would trump what anyone in this town would think once he and Violet told everyone that they were together.

And he'd do that soon. He'd said it before, but this time he meant it. After tonight, he definitely wouldn't care anymore about what everyone else would think or say about him and Violet, how much guff they were going to give him for stepping over the class divide in St. Valentine.

Davis pushed aside all those concerns about her father and his infamous dislike of the "richies." Pushed away everyone else, too, as Violet slid toward the backseat, pulling him by the shirt to follow her there, passion in her eyes, and something much, much more.

"I'm so in love with you, Davis," she said. "I never thought I'd feel this way about anyone."

"I love you, too," he said, as he lay her down in the backseat for what would be their first time. Her first time. "I'm always going to love you, Vi..."

Her voice brought him back to the here and now, in the Orbit Diner, sitting across from a woman with the same dark red hair, except it was shorter, sharper at the edges. A woman who'd somehow found another life without him.

"I wonder," she said, "if maybe going to L.A. with me would've been the easy way out for us." She said it carefully, as if she hadn't been able to afford thinking any other way.

He'd gone through the years with that protective attitude, too, and the excuses hadn't fit him. He realized that now.

"Why do you say that?" he asked.

She gave him a wounded look. "I was willing to tell my parents about us and to withstand all the fallout with my dad and anyone else in town who would've given me a hard time for dating above myself. But you…"

He fisted his hands. She was right. "Yes, I was slow in wanting to let our secret out of the bag, but I would've told everyone before we left St. Valentine, Vi."

"Right before we escaped to a place where we wouldn't have had to deal with what everyone else thought? Would that have been reality?"

"Out there, it wouldn't have mattered. You would've been you, and I would've been me. Nothing else would've come into play."

From her expression, he knew that might not have been the case at all. It was a teenager's point of view, and it was a shock to know that he still hadn't gotten past it.

Wasn't it possible that there were things even in L.A. that they wouldn't have been equipped to deal with, especially if they hadn't even been mature enough to face the music in St. Valentine?

"Davis," she said with a sigh, "for a long time, I told myself that I was nuts for thinking that you were embarrassed to be with a miner's kid. I made up so many reasons you wanted to keep us undercover."

He held his silence, having no defense.

"It's okay," she said. "At least, now it is. But then, we weren't old enough to be running off together, and I think we both know that."

It occurred to him that he might be angrier with himself for how he blew it with Violet than he was with her.

It was so easy to think it'd been all her fault, and his mom's, but he'd been just as responsible.

Violet went on: "Besides, you wouldn't have been happy in a city. If the years have proven anything, it's that you're devoted to St. Valentine. Leaving it *would* have mattered in the end. From what I heard, you even turned your back on a life in Chicago to come to St. Valentine and play savior for the miners. And you settled here."

Yet he'd done it out of guilt for what his investigation had done to the town, he thought. Or was it something more than that? Had he stayed because St. Valentine was in his blood?

But once he'd thought Violet was, too.

"Maybe," she said, "you would've even come to resent me for taking you away from this town, or putting a rift between you and your mom."

"That rift would've happened, anyway." He arranged his face so that it didn't give away any emotion. After all, Violet was still the woman who'd accepted his heart only to throw it right back at him, no matter what he'd done to warrant it. "Mom hardened after my dad died. I was only four, but I knew, just by looking at pictures of them, how happy she used to be, how...soft. If you hadn't brought on a rift, then it would've been something else."

And maybe if he'd made different decisions, their relationship would've withstood his mom, but he didn't dare say so. He didn't even know why the hell he'd asked Violet that idiotic question about the future in the first place.

His smartphone rang, and he grabbed it from the holster on his belt.

Did he finally have that closure *now*? Had this conversation accomplished anything but dredging up old pains and maybe even some new ones?

The question lingered in his mind as he read the ID on his phone's screen.

He'd made arrangements to go to a "final planning meeting" that Lianna Hurst was throwing tonight in her three-story Tuscan-style villa for a Helping Hand Foundation barbecue tomorrow. Everything about the charity event was already finalized, but Davis knew that Lianna was more interested in having a private session with him than anything else, and he'd accepted the invitation before Violet had appeared out of the blue yesterday.

"You can answer your phone if you want," Violet said, as it rang again. Her voice was unsteady, and it weakened him.

But he didn't need weakness of any kind.

He put the ringer on silent, sliding the phone back into its holster. Maybe he should go to Lianna's and forget about how he should've just kept his mouth shut tonight.

He hadn't noticed when their waitress had brought them drinks, but he took out his wallet and left way more money on the table than the bill would require.

"Something's come up," he said brusquely.

"Oh." Violet glanced at her Cherry Coke, as if yearning for just a sip, but then Davis wondered if there was more to her expression.

Had they finally been getting somewhere? Was he wrong about leaving?

Ridiculous, he thought, getting out of the booth. There was no *where* with Violet. He had to remember that.

"You have a ride back to your place?" he asked. "Because I can—"

"I'll go home with my parents. They're still at the restaurant."

"I'll walk you there."

They passed the old men at the counter with their chess game, and Violet didn't say a word. Not until they went out the glass door with the tinkling bell and into the summer night, with its soupy air and cinder-hued sky.

"I can make it to the saloon on my own," she said.

"Of course you can. But I'm still going with you."

"These aren't the mean streets of L.A."

She was being very Violet—reacting to his mood, standing up for herself because of his sudden coolness. He almost smiled at her spit and vinegar, but it didn't seem like good timing.

They walked in scorched silence past the jewelry store, which was even now run by Judah White-feather. He didn't see them while he arranged his best turquoise pieces in a display case. Ahead of them, the hotel loomed, with its balcony and the ghosts of a 1930s gentleman and a good-time girl that were said to haunt it.

So many things in this town…haunted.

Along the way, everyone but the few tourists present were giving them strange looks. Stunned looks, actually, because no one would've ever predicted that they would see Davis Jackson and Violet Osborne together again.

Their breakup had been well-known, the fallout barely there—a story quickly forgotten.

As Violet stepped up onto the boardwalk in front of her family's restaurant, Davis thoughtlessly reached out a hand to help her up.

The second he made contact with the bare skin of her arm, an explosion rocked him, and he was sure she felt it, too, because she pulled away just as rapidly as she had last night. He let go quickly—reluctantly.

It just seemed so right to touch her.

"Good night, Davis," she said, already heading toward the swinging front doors where the sounds of a jukebox wove through the air.

"Good night, Violet," he said, although he suspected she didn't even hear him as she disappeared into the noise of the bar and grill, leaving him in the shadows.

After Davis pulled the Aston Martin into his car barn—which gleamed with everything from vintage Bentleys and Ferraris to new Jaguars and Maseratis— he stalked toward his mansion.

Most of the time, it was easy to appreciate how the moonlight slanted off the man-made pond that fronted the 14,000-square-foot abode that he'd purchased with dividends he'd made off investments from his trust fund. The mansion was constructed of stone, high windows and balconies. Lloyd Callum, his personal assistant, called it his "Fortress of Solitude" in a light tone, although Davis sure felt the solitude tonight.

Off in the distance, he heard a truck's engine roaring, probably some hands who were driving away from the nearby stables. Davis thought of going over there, just to see if there was any hay that needed moving or horses that could use some attention. Work never hurt when it came time to clear his head, and maybe the guys would be up for some beer and socializing.

But he actually wasn't feeling all that sociable or fun. Going to Lianna Hurst's hadn't been very appealing in the end, and he'd texted her about not coming to her planning session. Not even the playthings in his mansion—a media room full of collectible video games, TVs and foosball tables, as well as the Romanesque pool out back—tempted him.

He'd never really thought much about why he'd built this oversize house and stocked it with such amusements. Not until now. Had he been that bored? Hell— had he been trying to fill *himself* up because there wasn't anyone like Violet around to chase away the emptiness?

He entered his front door and, like the prescient wonder Lloyd always seemed to be, the right-hand man met him in the foyer, there to take Davis's suit jacket.

Davis gave it over, saying, "You know this isn't in your job description."

"You were probably going to toss it over some sofa or chair, and then it'll just have to be cleaned up," Lloyd said. He had a faint East Coast accent to go along with his slicked-back dark hair and laugh-line-rimmed eyes, although Davis had never been able to pin his employee down to any particular area of the U.S.

"Davis," he said, stopping him. "You should know that you've got company in your lounge. Your mother's been waiting for an hour."

Aw, hell.

Davis unbuttoned his collar. He didn't have to guess why his mother was paying a visit.

He went to the lounge, with its graceful stag-horn chandelier, a fireplace with an artful iron screen, leather furniture, high rafters and long windows that overlooked the pond and the deepening Texas night.

His mom was standing in front of one of the windows with her back to him, an etched crystal glass in hand. Her silhouette was cigarette-slim, garbed in a white suit, her bleached blond hair done up in a chignon.

"So she's back," Mom said just before she turned around.

Davis went ahead and made himself a drink from the minibar—whiskey, straight up. "It must've killed you to have been out of town yesterday when Violet showed up. You probably would've been at the Welcome To St. Valentine sign to block her way in."

"I did no such thing when she paid sly visits to her family before now."

Davis hadn't known about any previous visits to St. Valentine from Violet, although it made sense. She had always been a family girl. But it pinched at him to realize that she'd probably been avoiding him during those trips, just as much as she was avoiding most other people in town.

He took a drink, waiting for his mom to say what she had really come here to say.

She didn't disappoint. "Why on earth would you have her working in the *Recorder* office?"

"You're the eyes and ears of this town, Mom. Surely

you caught last night's gossip about the Tony Amati look-alike."

"Yes." She wore an amused little grin. "He checked in to the St. Valentine Hotel."

"The look-alike?"

"I believe his name's Jared Colton. He's taken quite a liking to your favorite diner, too. He was there for breakfast and lunch."

Davis just held his glass, almost in awe of his mom's resources. These days she lived most of the time in Houston, running the natural gas operation, and he had no idea how she still kept her ear to the ground so efficiently from that distance.

Then again, she'd always been controlling. When she'd become the head of his dad's natural gas business and the mine after his death, she'd taken to them like a swan to water; she'd even brought Davis up to run the family enterprises one day. But he'd chosen to go in his own direction, to a journalism degree and then the job in Chicago. And when he'd returned to St. Valentine because of the kaolin mine story, she'd hoped that he was here to finally don his family mantle. He'd surprised her again, finding his own place in the community instead after he'd spearheaded the mine closure.

As he'd started his personal campaign to help St. Valentine's economy recover, their relationship had gradually improved, although things sure hadn't been perfect.

The years had allowed him to somewhat come to terms with what she'd done by lying to Violet, but now that his first love was back...

"Vi's working on a story." He wasn't going to explain more than that.

She sighed, the ice in her glass clinking as she walked away from the window and came to the minibar, refilling her dose of B&B. "You're reeling her in with a freelance job, aren't you?"

Yes. "No."

"I don't know what you're thinking, Davis—whether you're out for a night of sweet revenge with her or a... God forbid, I don't even want to imagine that you might be thinking of taking up where you left off with her."

"Either way, it's none of your business, just as it wasn't fifteen years ago."

"You were a boy fifteen years ago, and if I hadn't stepped in—"

"I would have what, Mom? Been happily married to Violet? Have a family with her?"

His mom lowered her drink, the corners of her lipstick-red mouth drawn down. "Do you really think that's what would have come out of it, Davis?"

"We'll never know."

She set her glass on the minibar. "People change over the course of a lifetime. You both would've changed, even from the time you were teenagers to now. Why do you think the divorce rate is so high in this country? Because people marry before they're ready."

Sometimes he couldn't decide if his mom had become the ultimate realist after his dad's death or just a cynic. "I *had* done my changing with Violet."

This conversation was about as comfortable and

useful as the one he'd had with Violet earlier, and he walked toward the door.

"Davis—"

"Don't," he said, halting. "You overstepped your boundaries once. Don't do it again. Not when we've come this far with each other."

Her tone lowered, contrite now. "I just don't want to be telling you 'I told you so' in a few months."

"You won't have to." He held up a finger, emphasizing his next comment. "Violet and I are only working together, and it'll be no more than that."

Even the bullet of his last words sounded hollow as he walked out of the lounge.

The weekend crowd had come out for the annual Helping Hand barbecue that was being held to raise money for mining families who continued to struggle after the kaolin operation closure. Some of the families had never recovered, especially after the national economy had taken its own plunge, but it could never be said that St. Valentine didn't try their best to aid their own.

Although the Osbornes weren't exactly flush with cash themselves, they habitually attended the community-based functions that included both former miners and wealthier citizens, and today was no exception.

"I always take advantage of a day off," Mom said as she linked arms with Violet. They strolled toward the town square, from where the aroma of barbecue wafted.

Dad kept looking back toward the saloon. He hated it when his employees took over.

Violet pulled him along, too. It felt good to be braced

by her parents. She fully expected Davis to be at the barbecue, and she knew that there was probably no way to avoid him. But how long could she do that, anyway? Sure, last night had gotten awkward, with that conversation about what could've been, but she was still working on the Amati story with him. They were grown-ups. They could handle it.

A few teenagers had been recruited to be on "burro duty," keeping the legacy animals away from the barbecue area. Everyone else milled around the grassy expanse of town square, with its gazebo, benches and leafy trees. It was already getting hot, and there were a variety of sun hats shading heads, fans being fluttered in front of faces. Umbrellas had been raised over picnic benches, too, and misters had been placed in strategic locations.

"The Helping Hands think of everything," Mom said. She stuffed their donation envelope into the slit on a tall basket waiting near the entrance to the community area. "I'll bet Davis sprung for the misters and umbrellas himself."

As Violet had said last night, it was obvious Davis loved this town. Something like pride welled in her, but she didn't know why. She had no emotional stake in Davis.

Before she could investigate that thought too thoroughly, Mom greeted a table full of ladies from the Blue Belle Club. The elderly, elite socialites, who were clearly on "their" side of the barbecue, said hellos to Mom and Dad, although they acted as one would to waiters—polite but uninterested. They merely inspected Violet.

Dad muttered something gruff that Violet couldn't

quite hear. But then he spotted a group of friends across the square, near the smoke-laced grills. They were former miners—a crowd that had supported Dad in reporting the mine conditions and causing Davis's investigation.

Luckily, most of the workers who'd despised Dad for his so-called betrayal were off in the natural gas fields near Houston now, and their families stayed to their own side of the barbecue, too.

Dad's buddies waved to him, and he returned the gesture.

"Go on over," Violet said. "We'll be fine."

Mom agreed, sending Dad to his friends as she stood by Violet.

"The same goes for you," Violet said. "I see some old high school friends I want to visit with."

Friends was probably being generous, since a couple of them had been on her newspaper staff, but Violet hadn't kept in touch with them. Too bad her best friend from school, Rita Niles, was out of town. It would've made the social scene here much easier.

An amiable voice saved her. "Well, look here. Just who I've been waiting for!"

It was Wiley, and he was in his full silver-haired glory, with a plastic cup in hand. He waved it around, indicating the festivities. "Isn't it exactly how our town founder would've wanted it? Everybody helping each other."

True enough. From her research, Violet at least knew that after Tony Amati retired from the Texas Rangers in the late 1920s, he'd bought land near the spot where St.

Valentine would be founded, and it had produced oil. He'd used that money to support families after the town's establishment and during all the hard times, especially on his ranch, where he employed everyone he could.

The property had been sold off and converted into apartments years ago; otherwise Violet would've already gone there to poke around.

Mom nodded toward a far table, where her bunko club sat. "Do you mind?"

"Not at all," Wiley said. "Right, Vi?"

"Right." She kissed Mom. "Have fun."

And she was off, leaving Violet with her former mentor, who wasted no time in steering her toward the gazebo, in spite of all the stares—*and* the way everyone looked at each other afterward, as if they were rolling their eyes. Giving each other the "why is she even bothering to show herself?" faces.

Too late, she saw Davis in the middle of the structure, looking into an open box and frowning. He was dressed casually again—a Western shirt with its sleeves rolled up to the elbows, old and faded jeans that seemed to mold to his long legs. But he was still every inch a reminder of money and how it had once divided them.

"I believe a woman's touch is required here," Wiley said.

Violet almost skidded to a stop until Wiley laughed.

"Trust me," he said.

He led her up the steps, and the moment Davis saw her, his blue eyes lit up.

It shocked her, as if she'd touched an exposed wire.

Emotion sizzled through her—light, electric and dangerous.

"I've brought the cavalry," Wiley said, dropping her off just as quickly as he'd come.

Violet tried not to look at Davis again, but it was impossible not to. Damn.

She jerked her chin toward the open box. "What's giving you trouble?"

He grinned wryly. "Take a look."

She did, finding a tangle of what seemed to be long red, white and blue decorative ribbons in the box.

"I thought everything was in order," he said, "but I found a stray box that the committee really wants to put up."

"These decorations look like they'll be used next Friday instead of today."

"Oh, no, the Chamber of Commerce has bigger plans for Founder's Weekend. Huge bunting that'll stretch down the streets. None of this little ribbon nonsense."

Why did it sound as if they were comfortable with each other, as if last night's strained conversation hadn't happened?

As if she hadn't been mired in memories of being with him, body and soul, for hours afterward?

She pushed the memories away, pulling the box toward her and digging in to it. "I can wrangle these, then start hanging them up around the gazebo area."

A voice from behind her interrupted. "Your interest in community affairs is touching."

Violet would know that catty tone anywhere. When she turned around, she found Jennifer Neeson right behind her, looking every inch the glamour-puss that she had the other night in the newspaper office at that cock-tail party. This time, though, she was wearing a white dress, probably made by someone like Ralph Lauren, plus a tennis bracelet that surely cost more than Vi's rent back in L.A. Her dark hair was fixed in a low, elegant ponytail, and she bored a hole through Violet with her gaze.

"Jennifer," Davis said. "I think Lianna is setting out the playlist for the DJ. How about checking in there?"

The news drew Jennifer's gaze away from Violet. "*I* was in charge of the playlist."

Davis shrugged and went back to the ribbons in the box.

Jennifer sighed and walked off, and Violet caught Davis's subtle smile just before it vanished.

"That was a wicked trick," she said.

"What—did you want her to stay?"

"Not particularly."

As Violet pulled out a tumble of ribbon, Davis got se-rious. "I'll be damned if I'll stand here and see her sling insults at you, Vi."

She paused in her ribbon wrangling, warmth flowing through her at the grit in his tone.

Obviously regretting his show of hard emotion, he dipped his hand deeper into the box, as if to concentrate on this simple activity.

When he brought out his own bunch of ribbons, Violet's hand got yanked forward, because the ribbon she'd been grasping was connected to his.

Her fingers brushed against his hand, and fireworks

went off in her chest, then even lower, but she didn't pull away this time. Not after he'd just sounded so protective of her.

And when he slid his index finger over hers, all she felt like doing was taking the couple of steps it would've required to go to him, wrapping her arms around him.

Giving in to what seemed inevitable in this raw moment.

Chapter Five

An innocent touch shouldn't have almost brought Davis to his knees. But just the slightest brush of skin against skin was enough to turn his belly upside down, his chest inside out.

He looked down at Violet, her cinnamon brown eyes soft with an openness he hadn't seen since she'd returned. Questions, answers.

Could it work if we tried again?

Yes, he thought, in this moment. *Yes, it could.*

He could hear her breathing, and each inhalation swept through him, too. It seemed right to go a little further—to wind his finger around hers under the cover of all those ribbons, to link to her in such a small yet significant way.

Around them, it was as if everything and everyone

had stopped motion, stayed frozen in time while Violet and Davis caught up with each other in the Texas heat.

He wanted to kiss her so badly…

Then, out of nowhere it seemed, music invaded their bubble—tunes from the DJ stand at the edge of the square. Some kind of manufactured, autotuned pop that brought Davis out of this spell.

Violet obviously got shaken out of it, also, and when she tried to move away from him, just as she always did, Davis didn't let her.

He kept his finger curled around hers under the ribbons. "I heard you used to make short visits to town, and you never let anyone know. Were you trying to avoid me all that time?"

The ribbons rustled, tickling his arm, making him a little giddy to know that she hadn't run off from him just yet.

"I only came back to see my parents and Rita and her daughter. I wasn't actively avoiding you," she said, side-stepping his question. "Besides, it wasn't as if people were clamoring to see me, so I stayed out of the town itself."

When she glanced up at him again, he saw the vulnerability in her—the former woman-who'd-had-it-all who'd lost the job that defined her, the one who'd had to slink back into St. Valentine to recoup her resources and maybe even her confidence. The one who probably thought he still had anger bottled up inside, all because of her.

He'd give anything to see her on top of the world again.

In the background, the music abruptly changed from pop to a Keith Urban song. Davis became ultra-aware that he and Violet were still touching each other under the ribbons. Violet realized it at the same time, and she finally unwound her finger from his, moving to the other side of the box and grabbing another bunch of gnarled decorations.

It was over…for now, Davis thought. But he'd seen a lot in her this afternoon—things she probably hadn't meant to reveal. Enough to make him think that there was a reason fate had seen fit to bring Violet back to St. Valentine.

Back to him.

But did he have the strength to put his heart out there again? Was it even the same heart as before, when he'd been young and hopeful, too crazy in love to know what life might do to break it?

After the music switched back to the pop song, Violet looked toward the DJ stand, where Jennifer Neeson and Lianna Hurst were standing toe-to-toe, clearly unhappy with each other.

Violet laughed, but it was a little forced. "I remember when those two were vying for captain of the cheerleading squad. The competition never really ended there, did it?"

Davis wasn't about to get into just how the women had competed with each other since high school. After he'd come back to town, he might've had a little bit to do with their competitive streaks.

After Violet, he'd always made it clear that he wasn't

up for permanent grabs—not for Jennifer, Lianna or anyone who agreed to his noncommittal style.

Violet was giving him a knowing glance. She was on to him, as usual.

He shrugged, and she seemed to be waiting for him to deny her suspicions.

Always the playboy. That's what she had to be thinking.

How could he change her mind?

They continued to untangle the ribbons, and he wished it was this simple to untangle everything else between them. During the silence, his thoughts even became a mess—was Violet wondering if he'd dated anyone seriously over the years? Had she already heard through the grapevine about how he had played a wide field?

And was she thinking that she'd been right to listen to his mom all that time ago, because he probably wouldn't have ever stopped his habits?

By the time the ribbons were ready to go, Jennifer Neeson's dad, the mayor of St. Valentine, had clearly settled the great DJ debate, and more hard-driving country music was playing. Over by the side dish table, where Jennifer had taken charge of doling out the food buffet-style, she looked smug.

"Point for the mayor's daughter," Davis said as Violet took up a handful of decorations and started to fix them to the gazebo railings.

"I noticed." She glanced toward the street, in the direction of the *Recorder* office. "When I'm off ribbon duty, would you mind if I used one of your computers to access the archives? I'd like to start interviewing tomorrow, but I want to firm up my questions and some research first."

Satisfaction whirled in the center of him. He had her for at least another couple of days.

Holding back a grin, Davis said, "That sounds fine. By the way, rumor has it that Jared checked into Rita's hotel."

"Sticking around, is he?"

"Strange, for a man who said he was only passing through."

When she smiled at him, it was one of genuine camaraderie, just like the kind of smile she would've flashed after he'd proved himself worthy to her on the high school paper. The kind of smile he'd seen before they'd first kissed and her smiles had started to take on a whole different meaning.

A ragged need tore through him, not only because he longed to prove himself worthy to her all over again, but because now, more than ever, he was determined to see her gaze melt whenever she looked at him.

Maybe he *was* out to prove to her, and himself, that he could still have her—just as his mom suggested. And maybe it was something else he didn't want to think too hard about right now.

But, either way, he wanted to win her over, come hell or high water.

The ride home from the barbecue convinced Violet that tomorrow, when her car would be out of the shop, couldn't come soon enough.

Her dad was currently at the wheel of their Ford truck, which bounced every time they hit a rut. He'd given Violet one wary look when he'd seen her come out of the *Recorder* office at the end of the barbecue and hadn't said a word since.

Mom wasn't so shy with her feedback. "No wonder you come off as antisocial, Vi. Working through the barbecue? Why?"

"It's no big deal. I put in an appearance, and I donated money and hung some decorations."

"And then you disappeared. How do you think that looks to everyone?"

"Like I'm working hard on the *Recorder* article. When they see it, they'll understand."

She hoped. Because, honestly, she probably hadn't won any favor with people like the Blue Belles today by skipping off to do her work. But she'd known that Davis would be busy at the barbecue, and that meant she could concentrate without him there to distract her.

She tried not to think about that moment between them this afternoon. The look in his eyes—that "He's going to kiss me" sensation that had sent the blood racing through her. Even now, her heart clamored so loudly that she was lucky her parents didn't hear it.

What would she have done if he *had* tried to kiss her?

"Well," Mom said, "at least you're on friendly terms with Davis."

"Too friendly," Dad piped in.

"Gary." Mom nudged him.

"Just saying my piece."

Right now, more than ever, Violet wished for L.A.,

where she wouldn't have anyone peering over her shoulder at every move she made. She loved her parents, but she loved wonderful, well-earned privacy, too.

When they got home, Violet wasted no time in retreating to her guest cabin, flopping belly down on the bed and inputting a number into her phone.

Rita. Violet surely could've used her old friend here today.

She knew Rita was helping out a cousin who'd broken a leg, though, and when she got her friend's voice mail, she wasn't surprised.

"Just want to say hi, and I miss having you here. Hurry home. Hope the caretaking isn't driving you up a wall. And give Kristy a big hug for me." Violet grinned at the mention of Rita's four-year-old sprite of a daughter as she hung up the phone.

Restless, she went to her bookshelves, where Mom had stored everything from textbooks for poetry and literature classes to high school yearbooks. She grabbed one of the latter and tossed it on the bed.

In the mood to talk, she dialed her best friend in L.A. "Hello?"

Just hearing Nancy's voice made Violet sigh. "Hey."

"Hey, yourself! What's going on?"

"Just got home from a rootin'-tootin' barbecue."

"Lots of Texas beef?"

Violet had told Nancy all about St. Valentine…and Davis.

She opened the yearbook to a page with Davis's color senior photo. She'd turned to it enough times so it was permanently marked, making it easy to look at him in his custom-made shirt and red tie, a cocky smile on his face.

"Hey...Violet?" Nancy asked. She'd also been on staff at the *Times*, except she still had a job as an associate features editor. "Are you okay?"

"I don't know what I expected when I came back here," Violet said.

"I do. For some reason, you were hoping that everybody would be different, and the years would erase what happened in the past. I told you it wouldn't be that way. Haven't you ever been to a high school reunion? Only the hairlines and dress sizes change." Nancy paused. "So... what's he like?"

Violet traced her fingers over his picture, her throat burning.

"Oh, that good, huh?" Nancy asked, filling the silence.

"Better."

"And...?"

And Violet told Nancy everything: about how angry Davis had been with her at first, about how he was trying—successfully, she hated to admit—to lure her back with the promise of a story. How she thought he might still have feelings for her.

Who knew what those feelings were, though? The remnants of a broken love affair? A burning need to right the past?

"None of it can go anywhere," she finished.

"Why?"

"Because I won't be here for the long run, and he

knows it. Why get involved, especially with a keg of dynamite, when I'll just have to leave again?"

Nancy was quiet, then she said, "That's sad."

It was as if she'd been hit in the gut. "Sad?"

"Sad that you wouldn't even consider that you *could* fall in love, and that you'd be able to work things out with someone you were meant to be with. Did he really do such a number on you?"

Now that Nancy said it, Violet wondered. After Davis, she'd never been able to fully commit to a man, had always told herself that she was swamped with work and there was no time for a truly serious relationship. Was there something more to it?

Or did it have everything to do with getting so damned beaten down by what she thought was love way back when?

Davis couldn't have mattered that much, but even as she tried to fool herself, she knew that he had.

And still did.

Violet rolled onto her back, staring at the blank ceiling and trying not to think about how empty it looked.

"At any rate," Nancy said, obviously knowing when to quit, "we all miss you here. The paper's been hell with a skeleton crew."

"I miss it, too."

"I'll let you know if I hear anything about an opening anywhere, okay?"

"Great. Thanks, Nance."

"All right. I hate to cut this short, but I do have a hot date."

And Violet didn't. But when she recalled the way

Davis had looked at her today, as if he were about to take her in his arms and press her against him, she tingled all over.

She said her goodbyes to Nancy, wishing her luck, then hung up the phone, picturing Davis's face on the blankness of the ceiling.

Filling her mind with an image that haunted her dreams all night.

The next morning, Davis was approving a digital layout of the *Recorder* when Violet came through the office door, flushed from being outside.

When she saw him, she took a breath, as if she hadn't anticipated him being here. But she recovered way before he did, his stomach still flipping with unexpected somersaults.

Did she remember yesterday, in the gazebo?

Did it even mean anything to her?

She held up a notepad, filled with scribbles. "Got my first interview. I would've loved to have caught our elusive Jared the stranger out and about, but he never seems to be around when I am."

"Maybe he sees you coming." Davis grinned. "Who'd you get?"

"Mrs. Ferris. She was outside the hotel on a bench, smoking a cigar."

Mrs. Ferris was the ninety-five-year-old town eccentric, who'd never cared much for convention. A perfect choice for Violet to approach first.

"How did it go?" Davis asked, trying not to dwell on

Violet's lush mouth and how much he'd wanted to taste it yesterday. And every day.

"She was nice, forthcoming, cordial. But all she had for me was old stories about how, when she was knee-high, she'd see Tony Amati driving the first car in St. Valentine through town. And how he preferred to ride his horse on the roads near his ranch so he could watch the sunsets." Violet furrowed her brow. "I guess he did a lot of sunset watching, and Mrs. Ferris has a romantic notion that he was actually watching for *someone*."

Davis could relate to old Tony. After Violet had shattered his heart, he'd done some sunset watching, but he'd been bitter, not romantic.

He stood from his desk and jerked his chin toward her notepad. "You do things old school, don't you?"

"I've got my system down. It's hard for me to concentrate on interviewing when I'm tapping on a palm keyboard. Besides, my shorthand is much faster."

He could tell by the bulge in her pants pocket that she used a PDA for recording interviews, though.

She nodded toward a computer. "Is it okay if I use one? Not for research, exactly, and I can transcribe my notes to my laptop at home. But I had an idea about something other than this Amati story…" She indicated the street outside the door. "During Mrs. Ferris's story-telling, she mentioned the days when cowboys used to gather in town. Some had poetry to read and music to play. She said it stopped when the silver mines around here got more popular and then got played out. And I guess the kaolin industry chased them away altogether."

"I remember hearing something about that."

"Well, since you're always thinking of ways to bring tourists into town… Wouldn't something like a cowboy poetry and country music festival each year be worth looking into? I thought I'd do a search to see how novel the idea would be around these parts."

It struck him that she'd been thinking of more than the Amati story. She'd been thinking of…him.

Was she starting to notice that he'd spent a lot of years trying to be worth something around here? That maybe the need for doing it was even rooted in the fact that Violet herself had thought so little of him all those years ago?

As she sat at a computer station, he told himself that he might be jumping to conclusions, so he settled down and considered her idea instead. And the more he thought, the more he liked what she'd had to say.

What would she, and the town he'd hurt by shutting down the mine, think of him if he could pull St. Valentine's economy out of the gutter with some new plans like this?

He leaned against a desk, watching her work. "There's a Chamber of Commerce meeting tonight at my place. They're descending on my house this week so we can brainstorm ways to make St. Valentine more appealing to tourists."

"You want to pitch them this idea?"

"Actually it would be great if *you* could do it."

When she whipped her gaze over to him, he held up his hands. "You should take the credit, Vi."

"With that crowd?"

The jab made him grit his teeth. Then he said, "So it still intimidates you—this social divide."

"No." She lifted her chin, as if showing him that her time in the city had taught her to become just as sophisticated as anyone. But then she seemed to remember his fancy cars, his hand-tooled boots, the pure silver belt buckle he was even now wearing. Rich-kid toys.

Toys she was a far sight from having.

He lowered his voice. "Just go home, get into your best cocktail dress and meet me out there. Do you know where I live now?"

"Who doesn't?" She pressed her lips together, as if thinking about her own reasons for wanting to help out the town, then said, "What if I don't have a cocktail dress here?"

Yes. "Did you put your things in storage in L.A.?"

"No. My parents had plenty of room for what I didn't sell off."

"Then you'll have a cocktail dress, city girl. Don't act like you don't."

Now she was frowning, and it occurred to him that she might not be worried about cocktail attire at all—in spite of her apparent confidence, she genuinely might be intimidated by the cocktail *crowd,* and any dress she owned might not live up to the likes of the designer duds Jennifer Neeson and Lianna Hurst would be wearing.

How could he tell her that she would outshine them all?

Something changed in her eyes—a true drive, a determination that was all old-school Violet. His chest rolled in on itself, squeezing.

"Okay," she said. "I'll be there."

He grinned, because he'd sure be waiting for her.

"Wow," Violet said under her breath, as she pulled into the circular drive in front of Davis's mansion.

All stone and windows, it reminded her of a massive, splendid hunting lodge for rich people. Her heart stuck in her chest, barely daring to beat.

Wow. Being here, seeing where he lived, really drove home how loaded he was.

A teen dressed in an ironed white shirt and black pants came to her door. The valet Davis had probably hired for the night.

She gave over her newly fixed Camry to him, shrugging good-naturedly as he checked out the faded red paint job. He grinned at her just before she went to the mansion's door.

She didn't even have to use the ornate iron knocker because the door opened, manned by a slim guy with slicked-back hair and welcoming eyes.

He gave her a wide smile. "Ms. Osborne?"

"You were expecting me."

"Davis told me to keep a special eye out for you. My name is Lloyd. I'm Davis's assistant."

"Thank you." She handed him her simple black wrap, then her dark, beaded clutch purse. She couldn't stop herself from pushing her hands down her dress, making sure there were no wrinkles.

"You look very Audrey Hepburn," Lloyd said.

This time she beamed. She'd hauled out her best cocktail garb, dressing with care in a black silk sheath with cap sleeves and buttons running down the low back until they got to a playful little bow. Her shoes were one of the few indulgences she'd once allowed herself on a modest salary—Jimmy Choo platform sandals that featured a dainty ribbon around the ankle.

Even from the foyer, she heard the murmur of conversation. Lloyd guided her toward the sound, outside on a plank-and-stone terrace lined by bushes and Chinese lanterns. The view overlooked an expanse of land and starry sky.

So this was where Davis went every night.

Refusing to dwell on what else he did at night, Violet took a breath and forged into the lion's den.

At first, the crowd didn't notice her arrival, they were so immersed in each other. But Violet saw Davis right off, dressed in a tailored navy suit that made her libido twirl, especially when his gaze met hers.

It felt as if she were being lifted out of her body, caressed by the stroke of his gaze…until she saw Jennifer Neeson and Lianna Hurst by his side.

One dark, one blond, both looking at Violet with barely veiled contempt.

Why did she feel like Cinderella when the stepsisters had seen her in her first dress, before the fairy godmother had come on the scene?

Davis excused himself from the women, and Violet didn't pay any attention to their reaction—she couldn't drag her sight away from him.

Tall. Broad-shouldered.

Oh, boy. Oh, *man*.

"Just in time," he said, his voice as much of a caress

as his gaze had been. "We were about to settle down for some brainstorming."

He gestured toward a huge glass-and-iron table with seats around it. Her gaze lingered on his long fingers, and she imagined how they might feel somewhere other than her hand.

Somewhere far more wicked...

Shaking off the thought, she allowed him to take her by the elbow and walk her to a seat at the end of the table. The patch of skin where he'd touched her burned, spreading all over her body.

As she sat down and looked down the length of the table, she realized that he'd put her in a place of honor.

He summoned everyone to their seats, and they put their drinks and appetizer plates on the table. Then he took the chair next to hers.

A brunette man, his hair longer than most, his skin whiskered, his wardrobe nothing more than flannel and casual jeans, assumed the seat next to Davis.

Davis introduced him to Violet. "This is Aaron Rhodes. He moved here about four years ago to open up the carpentry shop on Sunrise Avenue. He's also the president of the Chamber of Commerce."

"I don't know how I was talked into it," Aaron said, his green eyes sparkling as he stood up to shake Violet's hand.

When his grip lingered a second longer than it should've, Violet laughed and withdrew. Aaron grinned, too, and Davis rolled his eyes.

"Sit down," he told the man, and from his tone, it was obvious they were friends.

But when Davis glanced over at Violet, she saw something like possession tinging his gaze.

She shivered, and not unpleasantly.

From that point on, her mind raced, barely registering what Davis said to everyone—something about Chamber of Commerce, planning, hell of an idea…

Then everyone was watching her expectantly, especially Jennifer and Lianna from down the table.

Violet sucked it up. Why should she care about a pair of former cheerleaders? And who gave a crap if they were wearing Valentino and Versace?

She launched into her idea about putting on an annual cowboy poetry and country music festival in addition to St. Valentine's usual Founder's Weekend. Then she winged the rest of it.

"We could also attract people by having something novel in, say, the culinary field. A Western barbecue cook-off or a chuck wagon contest that would draw an enthusiastic, specialized crowd. And as far as yearlong attractions are concerned, why haven't we ever capitalized on the old silver mines? Calico Ghost Town in California uses theirs as a draw, and they have things like gunfights, the Mystery Shack and a working railroad, too."

Mayor Neeson, a squat man who had somehow miraculously produced his leggy daughter, said, "Davis mentioned the silver mine angle once."

"It was shot down," Davis said, grinning at Violet. Great minds thought alike—that was no doubt running through his head. "I believe someone said it was too much work to develop."

"I don't know who said that," the mayor muttered. "But it was before my term. I happen to like what I'm hearing now."

Aaron chimed in. "I like it, too. Let's get started on it."

Violet could've hit the roof, if there'd been one. The mayor wasn't dismissing the notion outright just because it'd been presented by *her?*

And when the man gave her a considering glance, she wondered if Davis had, perhaps, had a word with him about being open-minded. Or if she'd been just as biased as she'd assumed everyone else still was.

The rest of the meeting consisted of brainstorming how to institute a festival, who would research what, who would eventually be in charge. Davis took on the brunt of the work, and she found herself smiling at him again, admiring the man he'd become, and not just because he fit a nice suit all too well.

In the end, she managed to stay after everyone else had left—even Lianna, whom Lloyd gracefully lured out the door.

Davis shook his head and loosened his tie as he walked out of the foyer and into the seating area, where she'd been looking out a window. "I thought the night would never end."

"Why do I get the feeling that you were doing a little sweet-talking in some ears before I got here?"

He tried to look like he had no idea what she was going on about.

"Davis?"

With a maddening grin, he opened a sliding door to

the terrace, where the Chinese lanterns were still casting multicolored light. Stuffing his hands into his pockets, he lifted his gaze to the sky.

When she joined him, he finally answered. "I might've laid a bit of groundwork. I told you that I wouldn't tolerate any mistreatment of you."

"Thanks. It made things…easier."

He seemed surprised, as if he'd expected her to get feisty on him and scold him for meddling.

"You know," she said, "you've really got this town's ear. I think they'd be lost without you."

"You think so?"

Why did it sound as if her approval meant a lot to him?

When she'd left him years ago, she'd no doubt smashed his ego by questioning his worth. But it was ridiculous to even think that she was the reason he'd become such a leader.

Or that he wanted her to see the fruits of his labor now.

"After the mine shut down," he said, "I thought that most of the town saw me as a rich boy who was trying to throw around my money in an attempt to win their forgiveness."

"I don't get that feeling at all."

"Then maybe I've finally done a one-eighty from that playboy you knew way back when."

She looked down, then back up at him. She was so tired of always glancing away.

Their gazes held, and yearning sizzled through her.

Just say what you want to, she thought. *He deserves to feel good for once.*

"I'd even venture," she whispered, "that you've become a hero, Davis."

It was as if she'd opened a door—one that led to terrifying, wonderful things that she could barely see through the haze that scrambled her vision.

His expression changed, growing intense, shocking her system.

The next instant, he was closing the distance between them, cupping her face then lowering his mouth to hers.

Swept away, Violet allowed that door to stay open, even as she battled to keep hold of her heart.

Chapter Six

The kiss was all-consuming, taking possession of every thudding cell in Davis's body as he gently pressed his lips against hers, as if testing, anticipating that she might once again pull away.

But when she didn't, Davis's emotions came to a head.

Passion.

Need.

Maybe even some of the anger that had been pushing at him these last few days.

His kiss grew harder, more demanding. One of his hands slipped back to cradle her head while the other slid down to the small of her back, urging her closer to him.

Her breasts and hips crushed against him, and she sucked in a breath under his mouth. His gut tightened, encouraging him to continue the bruising kiss. Devouring, seeking, making up for lost time, he showed her just what she'd been missing.

Yes, he'd *wanted* her to notice everything he'd done for St. Valentine, even though he hadn't accomplished any of it for her sake. When he'd come back to town, his motives had been pure—he'd only wanted to redeem himself for getting that mine closed, and he'd put every effort into helping St. Valentine rise up again.

But now that Violet was back, Davis didn't mind being looked at as a hero—a man who was made of better stuff than what his mother had told Violet on that long-ago day that had changed their futures.

By now, she was pulling at his jacket lapels with a desperate grip. She made a small sound against his mouth, the vibration tingling his lips...

Too hard, he thought, easing up on the kiss. *Too fast.* But it was nearly impossible to fully back away from her, because he'd been waiting for so long, never knowing if he'd ever have this chance again.

A chance for what? Showing her that she made a mistake?

Or something else?

He lifted his lips from hers all the way, and she raised a hand to her mouth, as if the pressure of his kiss had left her lips pulsing and tender.

An apology twisted inside him, but he didn't voice it—he didn't have the chance, because Violet buried her face against his chest.

Instinctively, he rested a hand on the back of her head. Her hair...just as soft as he remembered. Long, gleaming, thick. The scent of it—cherries and almond—took him back to better times, when it'd been so easy to be gentle. To not just reach for her like some man possessed and taking what he wanted.

She finally spoke. "That was…"

Her words trailed off, and she stepped away from him, not far, but far enough so that he didn't feel the impression of her nestling against him anymore, the shape of her burrowing deep inside him.

"I'm sorry if it's not what you were expecting," he said, his voice graveled.

"Why did you do that?"

"I didn't plan to."

She pushed back her hair, almost nervously. "Oh, so you haven't been stringing me along, inviting me to work with you on the story and then to come here, to a Chamber of Commerce meeting? You never planned to get me alone during any of those times?"

"You were the one who stayed longer than anyone else tonight."

She rested a palm against her face, as if to feel the heat there. The blushing light from a lantern veiled her skin.

"You're right," she said. "I did stay longer than everyone else."

Night sounds hushed around them, expansive and yet far too intimate all at the same time. An intimacy he didn't deserve with her. That was agonizingly clear now.

"You're still angry about everything," she said.

His kiss had told her that. "I was trying to be anything but angry."

"But I felt it. It's unavoidable, that anger. And, believe it or not, I was the same way, right after I left St. Valentine. I was angry with your mother. I was angry with who we were, because it was such an issue between us. The fact that you wouldn't go public with us told me that." She swallowed. "I was angry with myself, too. And…"

A hesitation, then the words came rushing out. "I was angry at you for not understanding that I was only human for listening to your mom, even for the slightest second of doubt."

He understood every bit of it now, all too well.

He wanted to kiss her again, showing her that he could get beyond the anger. Every inch of him was dying for her, pounding, growing hotter and hotter with every passing second, and he almost reached out to take a lock of her red hair between his fingers, to trail his fingertips down her neck to rest on her delicate, perfect collarbone in a prelude to what could be between them now.

But she had already crossed her arms over her chest. "Why would you even kiss me when you know I'm only going to leave again?"

He didn't have an answer. Was there something warped about him that was setting them both up for a repeat performance of the past? Just imagine: them, falling for each other again. Her, having to play the part of the bad guy once more, abandoning him when he'd known for damned sure this time that she had always planned to leave.

Why would he do that? He had no right to expect her to stay this time. So why *had* he kissed her, starting things up again?

"It was impulsive," he said. "I'm sorry I did it."

But he wasn't.

"So you just had an itch to scratch." Now *she* was the angry one. "Wanting is what got us into trouble in the first place. We were so arrogant. We thought we lived in this bubble where love would keep us cozy and safe, and when it burst, we were somehow surprised."

"Funny," he said, her words needling him. "You used to believe in true love."

"I was too young to know better. So were you."

"Then why—"

He cut himself off because he'd been about to say something lethal.

Then why am I still feeling it?

But the truth was that he didn't know what he was feeling right now.

"Why what?" Violet asked, her voice tiny. She was daring him to go on.

But he wouldn't. Maybe she was right—it could've been that what they'd felt for each other was just hormonal, an illusion sparked by a good-girl-bad-boy teen dream. But they'd grown up, and adults like them should know better now.

"It's nothing, Violet." He straightened his jacket, then turned toward the sliding door, silently telling her that it was time for this conversation to end.

They went inside his mansion, and he fetched her wrap and clutch bag from the coatroom. The valet had already brought her car around the front, and she left while Davis stood in his doorway, watching her taillights disappear into the night.

Closure, he thought. He should've had some by *now*.

Then why did it feel as if he'd laid himself more open than ever tonight?

The days dragged by as Davis went about his business—overseeing publication of the latest edition of the *Recorder*, taking it upon himself to mend some fences on the ranch, managing his investment portfolio and the dividends that kept his funds liquid. He even skipped town for a couple days, flying in his private plane, a Gulfstream that he stored at the nearby small airstrip, to Miami for the opening of a new boutique hotel he'd invested in.

He also managed to see to the details of the upcoming Founder's Weekend, keeping in touch with the mayor, his assistants and even Aaron by phone and email.

But none of it was enough to make him forget that kiss.

In his fantasies, he swept Violet away, using his fingertips to map the beauty of her face—from her temples, to her cheeks, to her full mouth. He seduced her with soft words, planting little kisses at the corners of her lips until she smiled. He felt every inch of her against him, excited and so willing to forget their history.

Every remembrance was anguish, keeping him up at night, unable to be erased by *any* amount of work and distraction. It was bad enough that Violet was still working on the Amati project. True, she contacted him only by email to update him on the interviews she was conducting with the old-timers around town who provided plenty of historical color yet nothing enlightening about Amati, but…

But it was torture to know that she was so near yet so far. Still, Davis thought that he was probably even lucky that she was at least sticking to her word about finishing this freelance article for the town's sake.

By the time Founder's Weekend rolled around, he was back in town, hardly expecting to see Violet pop by the newspaper office when he was there or to run into her on the street during the hustle and bustle of preparing for the festivities. He was sure she would be doing her best to avoid seeing him face-to-face. Hell, he didn't even know what they'd say to each other on a personal level now, since he'd blown it so spectacularly with her.

There was a Friday-night buzz in the air—anticipation for the weekend. The St. Valentine Hotel was fully booked, and a couple smaller venues in the new town took care of the overflow, although they still had vacancies. That part concerned Davis; he'd been hoping for a bigger crowd this year.

When he dropped into the Orbit Diner for something to eat, there was no seating available except for the Formica-topped counter, next to the plastic-bubble-encased pies and the cash register.

But then he saw a man wearing a black cowboy hat low on his brow, sitting next to an empty stool. Jared Colton, the Tony Amati look-alike.

Davis decided that tonight might be a good night after all.

As people around him belted out greetings, Davis

returned them, then slid onto the upholstered seat and didn't even bother to look at a menu.

The waitress came over, and he ordered a draft beer plus a Galaxy Steak Sandwich with Rocket Fries. The buxom blonde, whose pink uniform hugged her rounded hips, wasn't familiar to him. He glanced at her name tag, which read Annette.

"New in town?" he asked her.

"Here about a week. I just got hired, but I've got plenty of experience elsewhere, Mr. Jackson."

So she already knew who owned the place.

When Annette strolled away, Davis noticed that Jared the stranger followed her with his dark gaze, even though he did his best to hide it under his hat. Davis had culled a few other details about the man the first time he'd seen him in the Queen of Hearts: his laconic way of communicating, how he wore worked-in Wranglers and a pair of modest boots along with a heavy belt buckle that looked as if it'd been a prize from some sort of championship.

A rodeo cowboy. Davis had come up with that tidbit during a search.

"Ready for the weekend?" Davis asked him, making small talk with the man who could provide for the one and only interview Davis really wanted. Now that Violet had distanced herself from him, he was focused on Jared for the story that could possibly provide a narrative for St. Valentine—and provide a boost to the tourist trade.

Jared sipped from a white mug of black coffee. "I haven't really thought about the weekend."

"You're lucky you've got a room. I hear the St. Valentine Hotel is sold out."

"Didn't notice."

What the hell did this guy spend his time doing all day, if not noticing what was going on around him?

"You don't care about all the tourists?" Davis asked. "Because that's what Founder's Weekend is geared toward. There'll be pie baking, cider making, a burro race, Old West actors dressed as historical interpreters…"

"Not really my thing."

"Then what's the appeal of St. Valentine for you?"

Jared turned a slow gaze toward Davis. His eyes were as black as charcoal, and there seemed to be a burn behind his irises.

"This town is a good place to stop for a while, that's all," he said, turning back to his coffee.

Annette the waitress whisked by to drop off Davis's beer and refill Jared's brew. Much to Davis's shock, Jared offered a smile to her. It changed his face from stoic to downright…

Bright?

Was that even the word?

Annette winked at him and went on her merry, hip-swiveling way. Jared's gaze followed her again, but then his smile faded, as if he remembered…something.

As if he had his own hauntings, just as Davis did.

Violet's face eased over his mind, slipping down through him—his chest, his belly, lower…

Snapping out of it, Davis told himself to concentrate, and he made a mental note to sit down with the new waitress to see if she had any insights into this Jared character. After all, it looked as if she could've waited on him before.

But he was determined to give the man one more try on his own.

Just imagine what a story this would be, Davis kept thinking. *What a tale for St. Valentine to tell and profit from.*

"If you don't mind my asking—" he started to say.

Jared stood, laying down enough bills to cover his coffee habit. "I mind, Mr. Jackson. I mind a lot, and I know you're the owner of this town's paper. I don't have anything to say on the record in addition to what good coffee this place serves."

He glanced down the counter, to where Annette was chatting and smiling with George Manderly and Dexter Lars, who were at their seemingly never-ending chess game again. She lifted a hand in an amiable farewell and, with a tip of his cowboy hat, Jared was gone.

Davis stayed in his seat for a moment. Frustration was creeping up on him, and it wasn't only because he was spinning his wheels with this story. Everything seemed to be running into dead ends with him.

And that included a certain redheaded reporter he was still aching to see, no matter how hard he tried not to.

Bright and early the next morning, as the town was setting up for the first day of Founder's Weekend, Violet navigated the tents along a blocked-off Amati Street, checking out the artisan booths that would be selling everything from leatherwork to calico crafts to cotton candy and pottery. Later today, the burros would even be running a race, and the event would come to a climax with a dance marathon.

She would be working in the saloon since her parents expected more of a crowd than usual, although rumor had it that there didn't seem to be as many tourists as in past years.

But, since Violet had come up with a few ideas to drive up tourism in St. Valentine, she was actually optimistic today. And the Chamber of Commerce's reception of her ideas put a spring in her step, too.

The only thing that had weighed her down recently was that kiss from Davis and their revealing talk afterward. Then again, whenever she thought about the kiss—how his lips had felt so warm, how being in his arms had felt so damned natural—she was a girl again. An innocent who saw everything in a different light.

How could she be happy and down at the same time?

She couldn't decide *how* she felt about Davis anymore.

Up ahead, the hanging sign for the *Recorder* swung in a slight breeze that only halfway chased the growing humidity away. She prepared to walk right on by, but, damn her, at the last possible second, she peered into the window.

And there he was.

His back was to the door as he spoke into the speakerphone on his cell. He was wearing those faded jeans that cupped his rear end ever so nicely.

Why did the man have to look so good besides everything else she was struggling against?

She waited there for a second, realizing that this was ridiculous, staring at him through the window, just as she'd done on the first night of her return, wanting him, telling herself that she was a big girl now and he shouldn't intimidate her.

It'd just been a kiss, she told herself for the thousandth time. One little kiss. Why should it have this kind of power over her?

Well, she wasn't about to let it.

When she opened the door, he turned around. The male voice on the other end of the line was chatting about stocks, but Davis didn't seem to be paying much attention.

Nope, his eyes were fixed on her, laser-blue. Breathtaking in what they did to her.

"Lloyd," Davis said, knitting his brow. "I trust your judgment on this. Buy what you think I should buy."

Lloyd had barely signed off before Davis touched his phone screen and lowered his arm to his side. His dark blond hair was mussed, as if he'd been running his fingers through it in agitation, but it reminded Violet of days when they'd gone swimming in the creek, as far away from civilization as possible in St. Valentine. The wind would have blown his hair dry, leaving it heart-grippingly disheveled.

Miss me? he would've said, coming to their blanket, where she would've been reading a paperback, wishing he'd stop swimming and come on over to her. Then he would've kissed her, far more gently than he had the other night, with far more tender intentions...

"Hi," she said, knowing she could get the upper hand back with him. With *herself.*

"Hi." His eyebrows were still knitted. "I didn't expect to see you."

"I heard you've been out of town and…busy. Same here."

"I could tell by those emails you sent me about the interviews."

She motioned to his phone. "Bad day on the market?"

This idle talk was the worst. But everything major they had to say to each other had already been said, hadn't it?

He shook his head. "It's a good day, actually."

"Oh. It's just that…" She gave a narrowed glance to his hair and how out of sorts it was.

He ran his hand through it. "Yeah. Well, frustration comes in a variety of forms." He paused, then seemed to make up his mind about going on. "This morning, I got some projections for Founder's Weekend attendance, and they aren't what I'd hoped. It wouldn't be so bad if we were getting anywhere on this Amati story, but—"

"I know you were hoping something big would come of that." And that it would lead to a legend that would get St. Valentine's out of the red. "But I'm still digging."

"I've been working some angles, too. I ran into Jared Colton at the Orbit Diner last night."

Her pulse jumped. A break?

No—not if she could judge by the state of Davis's hair.

"He's a real closed book," Davis said, "and I don't think we're going to get squat out of him. I thought I could dodge that by talking to one of the waitresses he seems to get along with at the diner, but she told me that he doesn't say a lot to her or anyone. He just sits there and drinks his coffee and watches the TV over the counter."

"He hasn't talked to anyone else in St. Valentine?"

"Not that I know of. But I hear that he leaves his hotel room and drives out of town every day."

Davis must've found that out from someone like Mrs. Ferris or the old men who liked to sit in front of the hotel smoking.

"I could follow him sometime," she said, waggling her eyebrows. Literally chasing a story sounded like great fun.

"You're welcome to do it if you can manage to be a supersleuth. On these country roads, it's pretty easy to spot a tail."

"I'd still like to try." Maybe she could even recruit Mrs. Ferris to keep an eye out for Jared's vehicle from now on, letting Violet know when she would have the opportunity for chasing.

"What does he drive?" she asked.

Davis described the man's green Dodge, then went on. "We knew he was a rodeo cowboy from those internet searches, and I'm afraid that's all I still know."

"I'll look for more when the festivities are over. I'm afraid I'll be waiting tables until then."

By now, adrenaline was streaming through her, and the heat of her skin must've shown her excitement.

It took her only a moment to realize what was really happening here, though.

A team, she thought. Violet and Davis, together again,

working as if they had a connection she'd never felt with anyone since.

He exhaled roughly. "Sometimes I wonder if everything will ever come together."

For St. Valentine or with her?

She didn't dare ask. She just assumed that he meant the town, because it was less threatening that way.

"Why don't you forget about Jared Colton for today?" she said.

His laugh chopped through the room.

"Seriously, Davis." She went to the door and opened it. The sounds of the weekend's event—some happy shouting, the clatter of pottery from one tent, the murmur of music from a band warming up on the main stage in the town square—infiltrated the office. "Just come over here."

It looked as if he'd been longing for her to ask, and her body practically vibrated with need. But they'd played this moment out the other night—their bodies too close, their inhibitions down—and it hadn't been a fantasy come true. It'd been full of the reality of their breakup.

She would be leaving town as fast as she could, and she'd give Davis no reason to hate her again for doing what she needed to do. But they could be civil until then. Maybe even friends who could pin down the Amati story and revive their hometown.

Wasn't it possible?

Chest tight, she gestured for him to follow her. He did, his bootsteps thudding on the wooden floor, then the boardwalk.

The artisan tents fluttered in the breeze, and she

walked between two of the structures, guiding him to Amati Street. Here, some of the tourists had ventured out of the haunted hotel and were peeking into a tent that sold giant cinnamon buns for breakfast. Their aroma beckoned and Violet sighed.

"Tell me," she said. "Who was the person who ramped up Founder's Weekend like this? Way back when, it used to be just a few tents and an apple pie bake-off with Rotary Club tours through some of the older buildings."

"I suppose I'm responsible." He was grinning because he had to know where she was going with this.

"I should have known." As an amplified banjo started up a lively tune down the street, she jerked her head in that direction. "And the bands, the dance marathon tonight, the cowboy show tomorrow? Who thought of those?"

"Just don't blame me for the burro races."

"Davis…"

"Violet, I know what you're trying to do."

He was smiling, and maybe it was even the first real one she'd seen from him upon her return.

It had the intensity to whip her inside out.

Why hadn't any other man ever been able to do this to her?

"You always did know how to cheer me up," he said.

"Yeah, I did."

There'd been days when his mom had just about driven him insane with her overbearing ways, and he would come to school quiet and brooding. Violet had always known that Mrs. Jackson had been overprotective—everyone said it was a symptom of losing her husband so suddenly to a heart attack, and she no doubt thought that she could somehow save Davis from the unexpected, too, if she could just keep him in her sights.

Somehow, he'd come to stand close to her—close enough so that his shirt brushed her bare arm.

Goose bumps prickled her skin up and down. If she didn't lay down the law right now, she wouldn't have the strength to do it later. She'd barely been able to manage it the other night, at his mansion.

She tried to make light of their proximity. "If you need cheering up, I hear there'll be some rodeo clowns around during the burro race."

Her comment fell flat, but at least it got the message across. From the way he took a casual step away from her, she knew that for certain.

The distance, as short as it was, hurt. It even hurt that they were standing here together, and she would be going back to her real home in the city without him.

He surprised her then, extending a hand. "I get it, Vi. Friendship is the best thing for us."

"Yes," she said before she could think again. Before her goose bumps turned into something more serious.

Even so, she stared at his hand for a second, wishing...

No. No more wishing.

Grasping his hand, she shook it. "Friends?"

"Friends."

A million volts traveled up her arm, lighting her up, but then he loosened his grip, sparing her.

And making her hurt that much more.

Chapter Seven

After Davis and Violet let go of each other's hands, they said their goodbyes for the day, then he watched her walk through the aisle of tents.

Friends.

It was probably a good thing, because it meant they wouldn't be enemies. It was probably the most he should ask from her, too.

But it'd been such a long time since Violet had been the closest he'd ever had to a female friend that he wasn't sure he knew how to be that way again. He certainly hadn't been true "friends" with any other female afterward.

He headed down the street, through the growing crowd of homegrown attendees and the tourists. People stopped him to say what a great weekend this was shaping up to be, and it made Davis think of how Violet had wanted him to pay attention to what he'd done for the town, to feel some pride in it.

Amazingly, he did, maybe for the first time ever.

He passed the buildings decorated with bunting and the artisan tents on his way to the town square, where a banjo trio was plucking away at their instruments and drawing a crowd. Davis circled to the back of the performance tent, finding Jennifer Neeson and Lianna Hurst arguing about logistics for the apple pie bake-off, and he took a detour.

Over a week ago, before Violet came, he would've gone right over to them to flirt. But now?

It didn't seem that alluring. Violet made other women seem out of the question, even if *she* was off limits.

Friends, he reminded himself, as a weight sank within him.

Under the nearby gazebo, a group of older men—ex-miners—were seated in a circle, and Davis left Jennifer and Lianna behind to check in with the guys. He came around the back of the structure as they were talking and using their knives to whittle blocks of wood. A few handmade signs announced that they were selling their work, which perched on the gazebo railing—everything from little horses to woodland creatures and totems.

These men weren't exactly big fans of Davis's since they'd been forced into an early retirement due to the mine shutting down, but that never stopped Davis from being affable.

Their voices rose even above the banjos. "Have you seen him with that Osborne girl?"

They must've spied Davis roaming the square but

didn't know he'd come around to their area. He almost spoke up before they could say something they might regret, but he was too late.

"Well," said another ex-miner, "her daddy turned his back on us. Why wouldn't she do it, too, by hanging around another man who screwed us out of a job?"

They were talking about how Violet's father had blown the whistle on the kaolin mine's safety conditions. What burned Davis even more was that they were insinuating that Violet had inherited the title of "betrayer"—that she was a turncoat because she was friends with Davis, who'd attracted the Mine Safety and Health Administration's attention with his newspaper stories.

The third man chimed in. "I'll bet Violet Osborne learned a few things in the city—she's probably fast enough to keep up with Davis Jackson these days."

"He'll probably follow her anywhere now."

As they laughed, Davis sauntered from around the corner of the gazebo, picking up a whittled flower that reminded him of Violet. Her name and even her personality were as colorful as these painted petals.

At first, the men sat up straight in their chairs, then hunched over in sullen defense. One had a beard, one a long mustache, the other was clean-shaven. All averted their gazes.

"How's business?" Davis asked. On the outside, he was still friendly. On the inside, he was a mess of steaming ire.

The men weren't quite so bold now. The one with the beard, Trevor Thomas, answered.

"Things'll pick up."

Davis reached into his pocket for his wallet. "We could get some better signage for you to step up the traffic."

The men didn't say anything, probably surprised that Davis wasn't calling them out for their rude comments.

He leafed off a $50 bill from a wad of them as the ex-miners resumed their work with stiff, jerky movements.

"You know," Davis said, "it's been five years since the mine closed. Things have been tough since then, but everyone in this town wants what's best for its people, including me and, believe it or not, Violet Osborne. I'm sure you've heard about the article she's working on to develop St. Valentine's profile as a tourist destination."

They didn't look up from their whittling.

"Just to make my point clear," he said, his voice lowering, "Violet had nothing to do with that mine closure, and her dad was only looking out for you. I thought I was, too, and I never expected to hurt anyone."

Now Davis had their full attention.

The nice, helpful-guy persona had proven useful, but his time was over. "If you gentlemen have anything to talk to me about, you should say it. But Violet's a friend, and I won't tolerate any lies or disrespect for her."

When they didn't say anything, Davis tucked the money under a woodpecker on the railing to pay for the whittled flower.

"I think that should cover it," he said, referring to the money *and* his comments.

Davis began walking away, but not before he heard

Trevor say one more thing under his breath. "*Friends*, he says."

The men all chuckled, and for the first time in his life, Davis felt his skin flush. He'd said he wouldn't stand any lies about Violet, but the men had *Davis* nailed.

Even to the people who didn't know him very well, it was apparent that the whole "friends" thing was bull.

After the dinner rush ended at the Queen of Hearts, Violet was dead on her feet.

The customers had thinned, so she leaned against the bar, where her dad was tending to a visiting couple. Only about three tables were still full, and none of them were in Violet's section.

"You deserve a break," her dad said.

"We might get another rush."

"Doubtful." Dad frowned. "These just aren't the kind of numbers we were hoping for this weekend."

"But maybe—"

"I can handle what's left for a while. You've been working since morning. Why don't you go outside and have a little fun, Vi? You haven't seen a Founder's Weekend for years."

It was tempting, especially since she knew Davis was somewhere out there.

But she wasn't supposed to crave his company. Not with the law she'd laid down with him.

Buddies, she thought. *How's* that *working out so far?*

She pushed away from the bar. "Can I have a tea to go, Dad?"

"Coming right up."

He fixed it for her, pouring the beverage into a foam cup with a lid, the bag's tag dangling. She grabbed a packet of sugar and a stirrer. "I won't be too long."

"No hurry," he said, wiping down the bar.

She fought the tightness in her throat. Her parents had been depending on a healthy weekend to keep things going financially, and it was tough to watch Dad pretending as if his world wasn't crumbling.

She thought of Tony Amati, the look-alike…the story that could be picked up by TV programs like the *Today* show or some human-interest-centered magazines.

They needed the good press for St. Valentine, and the notion doubled her determination to help the town…and the people she loved who lived here.

Out of nowhere, Davis's face came to her.

After pausing, she shook her head, then erased him from her mind. Even so, she couldn't chase away the tiny shocks surrounding her heart.

She wandered onto the boardwalk, taking in the laughter from the street, the near distant country music from the small stage in the town square. The gas lamps were glowing in the dusk, lending a timeless haze to everything. St. Valentine was as beautiful as she'd ever seen it.

And when Davis Jackson strolled into her sight, it became even more so.

He was still wearing those be-still-my-beating-heart jeans, with a casual Western shirt, an outfit that belied the millionaire in him, except for the expensive, custom-made boots.

For a moment, Violet could only stare, her pulse flailing.

Friends. Just friends.

He strolled up to the boardwalk railing, where she'd set her tea before she could drop it. Her hands were actually shaking, dammit, so she held off on adding the sugar.

"Caffeine injection?" he asked, motioning toward the tea as he reached up and leaned his arms on the railing. His muscles strained against his shirt, firm and smooth.

"I'm getting my second wind," she said, smiling, telling herself that he did nothing for her.

And utterly failing.

"Knowing you, you'll have a third and a fourth wind before the night's over," he said.

"True. You might even see me in that dance marathon."

He lifted an eyebrow, and the gesture was slightly rakish, fluttering her pulse.

"You need a partner for the marathon, Vi."

Okay, time to scramble on to a safer subject, because he had a look in his eyes…A gleam that said he wouldn't mind holding her in his arms all night, moving with her around a dance floor.

"It was just a joke," she said. "I'm not much for dancing."

"You never were."

She narrowed her gaze at him. "Sure I was."

"Not as I remember it. If you were at a dance during high school, it was because you were snapping pictures or writing an article about the social scene."

"Well, I *wanted* to dance. I was just too—"

He said it just as she did.

"—busy."

They laughed, and it was such a nice change from all the taut moments between them that she missed the sound when it finally faded.

She lifted the lid off her tea, steeping it with the bag.

His voice infiltrated her with its low timbre, like something hot and soothing washing through her body.

"Do you go dancing in the city?" he asked.

"I used to, with my friends. But the clubbing scene got boring. There're only so many times I could have a conversation with someone on a dance floor while we shouted over the music."

"See—that's not really dancing, Vi."

"Are you criticizing my technique?"

"I'd never do that."

The conversation had taken a turn into something veiled, sultry, and she almost fumbled the tea from the rail.

She calmly ripped open the sugar packet and poured it all in, stirring.

It looked as if he was about to add another innuendo-laden comment, but she gave him a "don't say a word" glance before he did it. They laughed again. Natural, as if they'd been doing it since…

Well, forever.

A warm glow suffused Violet as her gaze met Davis's. He was watching her with more than wanting or the angry hunger she'd seen in him before. Now, there was just…a wish?

The same one that was revolving like a sharp, multi-sided prism inside of her?

Footsteps on the boardwalk brought them out of their moment. The sound of high-heeled shoes.

If it was Jennifer again, Violet was going to—

"Hello, Violet," the woman said, and it wasn't Jennifer. No, this tall, slim, bleached blonde dressed in a cool light blue sheath was older, more sophisticated.

"Mom," Davis said, and there was a warning in his tone as he lowered his arms from the railing, his hands going to his hips to rest there in a second warning.

His mother leaned against a post, holding her stylish clutch bag in one hand. "What, Davis—I can't say hello? I haven't seen Violet since…"

The words curled off, as if in a mist thick with meaning.

Violet spoke. "Since you lied to me about Davis seeing other women. I think that's what you were about to say, isn't it?"

Mrs. Jackson laughed. "She really has grown up, Davis. The Violet I knew wouldn't have ever talked to me like this. She wouldn't have dared."

Davis said, "I think that's enough, Mom."

Violet had spent years despising this woman for what she'd done, and it'd all built to a head, coming out in a rush of words now. "If I didn't know any better, I'd say my being here is somehow threatening to you."

The other woman laughed again. "You'd like to think you're that special, wouldn't you? But the truth is, Violet, that you were never as good as you thought. A miner's girl. Did you truly think you had any sort of future with Davis?"

His boots thumped on the steps as he came to the boardwalk. *"Enough."*

Violet was eerily calm, even as her adrenaline fired away. "It's okay," she said, still looking at his mom. "She's never gotten over the fact that you have a mind of your own."

Mrs. Jackson stood away from the post, her posture ramrod straight. "Let me do you a favor, Violet. Let me tell you the honest-to-God truth. You're a novelty right now to him—a could-have-been fantasy. And if you think he's going to be paying you this much attention after he catches you, you're wrong."

Davis walked around his mother, placing a hand on Violet's back and trying to guide her away. "You don't have to listen to this."

"Why? She doesn't bother me," Violet said, standing her ground.

But his mom had already descended the steps, yet not without one last comment.

"You were never anything special," she repeated. "Not to him, not to anyone. That's why you're back here where you started, without much of a present or a future."

"Damn it," Davis said, starting to follow his mom into the street.

Violet reached out to grab his shirt, but she didn't say anything. Her throat was too raw.

Mrs. Jackson had struck home with her drive-by hit job, burying her comments deep into its intended target—right in the center of Violet.

Nothing special. A castoff from the world she'd tried to conquer. Jobless, nearly broke and still a social pariah—that was Violet to a T right now, and there was no argument against it.

But she wasn't going to show the damage—not in front of *her.* Or Davis.

After Mrs. Jackson had melted into the crowd, Violet casually let go of Davis's shirt and stirred her tea again, praying that he wouldn't see the unsteadiness of her hand.

"What she said was dead wrong." Davis's tone was serrated.

"I know it was." Sure.

"Violet." He took her by the hands, even if she was still holding the stirrer, pretending she had even the slightest interest in tea.

His skin seared into hers. "Anyone who sees you as anything other than a success is crazy. She was just pulling out anything that she thought would get to you."

And she'd done the job.

He used his index finger to tip up her chin so that she was looking into those blue, blue eyes.

"Tell me you didn't take it to heart," he said.

Violet forced a smile. "It's water off my back."

But it was more like she was carrying a new load, and it was pulling her down lower than she'd ever thought she could feel.

Davis was torn between confronting his mother and staying with Violet, who was acting as if she hadn't just been lacerated.

But, really, was there any choice as to where he wanted to be?

He wanted to hold Violet close, show her that his mom was wrong—that Violet *was* special. That she was a star at whatever she did, whether it was reporting or stealing his heart.

Good God, he wanted some payback, because watching Violet try to brush off the insults was killing him.

She cleared her throat, and he realized he was still holding her hands, out here on the boardwalk, where they were drawing stares.

Who the hell cared?

Disengaging from him, she picked up her tea and the discarded sugar packet, throwing the garbage away in a nearby can.

"Violet," he said again.

"It's done," she said, going down the steps to the street itself, where they threaded through the crowd. "Your mom said her piece. Big deal."

"It *is* a big deal." He caught up to her, taking her by the elbow. "Talk to me, Vi."

"And what would I say? That it was fun to be reminded of why I'm back here? That she wasn't wrong about most of it?"

She moved on, walking slower now, and he let go of her elbow. There was no getting through to Violet right now. She'd been flayed, and apparently the last thing she wanted was to rehash the drama.

So be it, he thought. But he wasn't dropping the subject forever.

They were still weaving through people, passing the

tents, heading toward the town square, which had gone quiet except for the mayor's echoing voice preparing everyone for the dance marathon. Maybe she wanted to take her mind off what had just happened by listening to the DJ's music and watching the contestants for a while.

It rankled Davis that she was blowing the confrontation off, as if talking to him about it was the last thing she wanted to do. He didn't like being set aside that easily—it reminded him of being discarded when she'd gone off to L.A. without him.

They came to the town square, which was bright with fairy lights strung through trees. A dance area had been roped off, and nine couples were there, listening to the mayor's instructions: hourly breaks for seven minutes, the last couple standing at dawn wins, although if they came to the end and there was no clear winner, there'd be a dance-off.

By now, it seemed as if Violet had flushed the incident from her mind as she sipped her tea, her gaze traveling the square.

"Next year," she finally said to him, "after the Amati story comes out, you won't be able to move, there'll be so many people here. There'll finally be something to tell them about old Tony."

Had she turned to optimism because it didn't hurt nearly as much as his mom's words had?

A male voice interrupted from behind them. "We could use more couples out there."

Davis and Violet turned around, finding Aaron Rhodes standing there. He'd pulled his dark, shoulder-length hair back into a band; his whiskers covered his angled face, and he seemed nothing like the president of the Chamber of Commerce.

"Looks like it won't be much of a contest as it is," Davis said, thinking that he'd get Violet to communicate with him later. Come to think of it, for a reporter, communication had never been her strong suit, even when they were young. Violet had always been good at wrapping herself up in her books and her academic pursuits, and that was probably why winning her over had been such a teenaged thrill for him.

Until it'd turned into a whole lot more.

Aaron's gaze had brightened. "I'm glad you agree that the field is a little sparse, Davis."

Next thing he knew, Aaron was pushing Violet and him toward the ropes, yelling to the mayor to wait.

"We've got a late entry!"

Davis glanced down at Violet, who was holding her tea in front of her like a shield.

"I've got to get back to work," she said, motioning down to the waitressing apron she was still wearing. The Queen of Hearts card logo stood out against the red-and-white-striped background.

Aaron undid the rope and ushered them through. "I saw Mabel Holloway around—she's one of your waitresses."

"She got off at three."

"Then, being a good citizen, I'm sure she won't mind covering for you if the saloon needs it. We've got to get more people out here. Your *town* needs you, Violet."

Davis chuffed as Aaron positioned them near the center of the floor. "Then *you* get your ass out here."

"I'm running this event." Aaron shrugged and took Violet's tea from her. "What can I say—volunteering has its perks."

"Social misfit," Davis muttered, even though he knew Aaron was anything but. If there was a man in this town who dated half as much as Davis, it was Aaron.

"I've got your entry fee covered, and Violet—I'd keep that apron on. We'll say that the Queen of Hearts sponsored you. Good advertising." His friend grinned as he sauntered away toward the judges' table to register them.

"Can he do this?" Violet asked.

"Shanghai us? I guess so."

"But—"

His pride had been dented already with the entire "friend" farce, then the failed conversation about his mom. Her protests were the last straw. "The town needs us, Vi."

He'd known that would get to her, and as Aaron went to the microphone and announced that there were still a few minutes left for late entrants to come onto the floor, Violet stood with Davis toe-to-toe.

"I know that when you set your mind to something you can be as stubborn as a donkey, so I shouldn't even bother to argue."

"I recall hearing something like that about ten thousand times from my editor on the school paper."

Her gaze misted, as if she were remembering those days, too. The flirting disguised as fighting, the "accidental" brushes of their arms while they laid out the paper, the time after school when he'd rashly kissed her and everything had changed...

Four more couples had come onto the dance floor, and the mayor announced that the contest was closed.

As he counted down to the start of it, Davis put his hands on Violet's waist. She closed her eyes, then opened them, seemingly in shock.

"Five!" shouted the mayor.

Davis drew her closer.

—"Four!"—

He reached over, finding her hand, lifting it to his shoulder.

—"Three!"—

Violet didn't move, as if she was wondering if there was still time to leave.

Don't go, Davis thought. *Not this time...*

—"Two!"—

She still had that look in her eyes.

—"One!"—

Then, it happened.

She rested her other hand on his shoulder. He could feel every finger embossed into him, every crackle of tension between the small space that separated them now.

The DJ put on "Dance Time in Texas," a fast George Strait song, and a cheer rose up from the crowd as the other dancers swung into action.

Davis smiled down at Violet, and she smiled back, all his for the time being.

He twirled her, and away they went, whirling, swinging in time to the music, Violet laughing in a soul-cleansing sound that lifted him high.

As they danced, him leading her in the steps she'd

either never really known or had completely forgotten in the city, they kept laughing.

The time passed in a whir while they two-stepped, line-danced, took part in another swing…

Then a slow song came on.

After a pause, they eased together, their breaths evening out, matching, as she wrapped her arms around his neck.

A melt of warmth and need flowed through him.

Perfect. They were so perfect together. Why wouldn't she see that when he so clearly could?

When she stifled a yawn, he realized that she was more tired than even she would admit. Yet she would never drape herself over him as another woman might've done, and she would never give in to defeat, whether it was in a dance marathon or her determination to keep a safe distance from him.

But by the end of the night, it was going to be different, Davis thought. Forget the "friend" idea. There was more here, and he wasn't about to let it go.

Hell, no—by the end of this marathon, he'd make sure that she'd be holding on to him, without caring that she had other plans outside St. Valentine once she got back on her feet.

Chapter Eight

Violet was trying her damnedest not to give in.

Leaning against him would be a clear signal to Davis that she couldn't afford. It would encourage him, sending him the impression that she was going back on everything she had stood for—making her own way out in the world, living up to her promise to her great-aunt Jeanne that she was going to pursue her dreams and live up to all her potential, whatever it took.

But, at this instant, as she moved to the beat of a song about needing you now, it felt as if all her dreams were tied up in a soul-searching, knee-buckling dance with her first love.

She held her breath as his hand rested at the curve of her back. He fit so well there. But why not anywhere else in her life?

"Looks like I was wrong," he murmured, his words

warming her ear, stirring the hair there and sending a cascade of delicious wanting through her.

"Wrong about what?"

"Dancing." He tightened his grip on her hand. "You've obviously done it many times before."

"You're just being nice." She would have been a disaster during the swinging and two-step if it wasn't for him. He knew how to lead her.

Always had.

He laughed, and it rumbled through his chest. Even a heartbeat away from him, she could feel the vibration.

"Vi, I think you were practicing with someone all these years."

Practicing. He wasn't talking about dancing anymore, and the territory he was treading was more than friendly.

She decided to be honest about this. "I wasn't a nun, Davis. You weren't a monk, either."

"So you've been listening to gossip."

"Is it false?"

"No." This time, his laugh was softer, right by her ear again. "A guy like me needs an appropriate partner for charity events, for grand openings. For company."

It felt as if she was running, her heart hammering, even though she wasn't getting anywhere. "I wanted company, too."

Had his fingers tightened in hers? "Anyone in particular?"

"Not…really." That wasn't quite true. "I told you I was busy. But there was someone else, I guess… A sportswriter named Jon. He was just as career-driven as I am. There were times I thought that things with him would take a turn for the serious, and I wasn't sure how we were going to handle that, but neither of us quite made it there. He ended up moving east about a year ago for a job at ESPN."

"You didn't mind?"

"I…" She pressed her lips together, then just came out with it. "It didn't break my heart. We weren't ever willing to commit to anything, and that said a lot about what we were to each other. As I said, he's a lot like me—myopic, focused to the point of oblivion sometimes."

Davis firmed his grip on her hand, as if he was claiming her in some way.

"That's good to hear," he said. "About how you're totally free now."

He swept her into the dance.

As she swayed with him, she thought how right this was—she never followed the beat like this with anyone else.

But why now?

Why at all?

The first hour had flown by, and after the song ended, the mayor announced a break. Davis didn't let go of Violet, and as the couples around them abandoned the dance floor, it was just the two of them standing there, still holding each other.

"Davis?" she asked, her heart in her throat.

He grinned down at her, and she saw a resolve in his gaze that hadn't been there earlier.

Tonight, it said. *No more dancing around the real subject; no more fooling ourselves.*

This time, he wasn't letting her get away, and a sense of panic mixed with excitement stirred her.

He put his hand on her upper back and guided her to the edge of the floor, where volunteers were waiting with water. A lot of the couples had plopped onto the ground, resting.

But someone was waiting for Violet and Davis.

"Still standing?" asked her dad, as he handed two sweating bottles of water to them.

Violet wanted to sink into the ground, right there and then, but Davis didn't seem so inclined. He accepted the bottles from Dad and handed one to her.

"We got roped in to this," Davis said, "but we're making the most of it."

Her father's mouth was in a tight line.

"Thanks, Dad," Violet said, hoping he wouldn't pull a Mrs. Jackson on them and start pointing out all the reasons they shouldn't be within speaking distance of each other. She unscrewed the lid on her bottle and took a swig.

Then, to cut the silence, she said, "Aaron Rhodes said he would make sure you were covered with the restaurant. You need any help?"

"We're fine." Dad's chin went up a notch. He apparently didn't want Violet to mention that this weekend would be a financial disappointment.

Pride. Her dad had so much of it. Mom had told her once that the Helping Hand Foundation had offered him assistance, but he'd turned them down flat. No way would he ever have taken a penny from the richies.

She had the same debilitating pride, didn't she? Not

necessarily about finances, but in so many other areas—like the one that had protected her, sending her into a working frenzy after she'd left Davis.

Dad gestured toward the ground. "Maybe you both should take a sit." Then, to Davis, "Make sure she doesn't overdo it. She has a tendency."

"I've noticed," Davis said. He was wary, as if expecting a replay from earlier, too, when his mom had come on the scene.

Dad sent Violet his own cautious look, pulling her aside. "Do you know what you're doing?" he whispered.

She smiled at him. "I'm okay, Dad."

More than okay, to tell the truth.

Then, after a moment of consideration, the lines around his mouth loosened, and he nodded at Davis. "You two kids have fun."

"We will," Violet said, hardly believing that there hadn't been some kind of explosion.

One last, meaningful glance passed between the men, and Davis smiled. A serious smile that told Dad Violet would be in good hands.

A truce?

What had Dad seen between her and Davis that had urged him to come to terms with the man he'd always held such suspicions about?

The mayor gave a one-minute warning, and Davis extended his hand to help Violet to her feet—feet that were sore but ready to dance again.

Inexplicably, undoubtedly ready to dance with Davis.

"That was interesting," he said.

"Yeah, I don't know what just went on, but let's consider it a reprieve."

Soon, they were back on the floor, in the middle of another fast song, laughing. Violet had definitely gotten her second wind.

And, as the night went on, she got her third, just as Davis said she would. Then her fourth.

Other couples had started dropping out around the three-hour mark, and by the time the night sky was at its deepest velvet blue, only four couples were left.

But it was as if time didn't matter to Violet or Davis—in any way.

In the end, at dawn, as she slow-danced with him, her head on his shoulder now, no distance between them, the mayor cut off the DJ and announced the contest finished.

Fuzzily, Violet realized that she and Davis were already the last couple standing.

There was applause from the early Sunday morning crowd as the mayor gave Violet and Davis little trophies, each with a happy, dancing couple silvered in glory. But the image faded under her eyelids as she leaned against Davis again, even though there wasn't any music.

She smiled, exhaustion overtaking her, after what might've been one of the happiest nights of her life.

She bolted awake.

The backseat of an old car...white vinyl upholstery...

And the sight of Davis pulling away from her, his hands up as he let go of the blanket he'd been laying over her and got out of the backseat.

"Sorry," he said. The sun was shining, making his

hair golden, burnishing his skin in half shadow. "Didn't mean to wake you up."

She assumed he'd been putting her in the backseat to sleep while he took her home. As she sat up and looked around, she saw that his restored Rambler Marlin was in a small paved lot near the newspaper office, surrounded by other vehicles.

Groggily, she started to fold the blanket that he'd tucked around her. "The marathon's over."

"Way over. I brought you here for some rest while I helped shut down some of the festival."

Then it came back to her—the trophies, then sleep taking her under after a long, long day.

But she was awake now, so she climbed out of the back and went to the front while Davis chuckled and assumed the driver's seat.

"I caught a ride with my parents," she said. "Do you mind taking me home?" She had an early afternoon shift, but she might as well get some sleep in her cabin.

He nodded and handed her a bottle of water. She drank from it. Energy zinged through her. Davis made her feel awake.

Alive.

He started the car, then drove her home, the radio on, reminding her of their long, wonderful night.

Magic. Or the closest she'd felt to it in ages.

She didn't want to think about how long it would last with Davis. Hopefully, it'd wear off soon so they could get back to the business of living. Last night had no doubt only been a flight of fancy, an indulgence she could get away with just this one time....

After he drove onto her family's ranch property, down the dirt road and to the main house, she asked him to pull in by her guest cabin.

She noticed her parents' truck wasn't in the driveway.

Davis cut the engine. Without missing a beat, he was out of his seat, shutting the door, coming around to open her side.

Gentlemanly instincts. Davis might have been a playboy, but he knew how to treat a girl. Maybe that was why he'd been so lucky with so many.

But, somehow, it seemed as if he'd only opened doors for her, and no one else mattered.

He took her by the hand, helping her out.

"I'd invite you in for coffee," she said, "but—"

"All right."

He was already on his way to her cabin, the gingham curtains peeking out the windows as if looking to see whom she'd brought home.

Presumptuous, wasn't he?

She grabbed her trophy, got to the door, then brushed by him as he waited on her doorstep. As they went inside, the scent of pine wood permeated the air.

"I think I've got a carton of orange juice," she said, going over to the minifridge near the porcelain sink.

She put down the trophy and got the juice out of the fridge, then reached for two small glasses from the cabinet. After filling them, she gave one to him and assumed a secure distance near the window, downing her juice in record time.

He drank, too, but she'd beaten him, and she turned around to put her glass in the sink.

His voice rumbled, making her haul in a breath, because he'd come up behind her.

"Are we pretending last night didn't happen?"

"I thought we made an agreement," she said. "Friends."

"'Friends' isn't working for me, Vi, and don't tell me it's what you want."

Before she could say that it was—why couldn't he just accept it?—she felt his hands on her hips.

She sucked in a breath, her chest constricting.

"There's something that's still there between us," he said softly. "Stop acting like there isn't."

Since the saloon had "sponsored" her she'd never taken off her apron, even through all the dancing. He began slowly untying it. The material loosened from around her, slipping until he pushed it away.

It slumped to the ground, the only sound in her cabin besides their breathing. She could feel the warmth of him on her neck, her spine.

Everywhere.

Unlike the other night, when he'd kissed her with such fierce hunger, he was tender now, coaxing his hands to the front of her, where he laid his palms against her belly.

Her muscles jumped there, lightning striking lower, between her legs. Automatically, she laid her hands on top of his, as if to stop him, although she knew she wasn't going to. She couldn't fool herself anymore into thinking that she even wanted to.

What the hell was she *doing?*

When he nuzzled aside her hair to press his lips against her neck, her legs almost gave out from under her, and she grabbed onto his hands.

"This is a terrible idea," she said.

"Worse than lying to ourselves?"

He kissed her again—the sensitive area between shoulder and neck, upward, to the spot right behind her ear.

Her knees buckled. He'd always known where she liked to be touched. No one else had ever been so in tune with her. No one else had ever made her respond like she was doing now, reaching back, cupping the back of his head, encouraging him.

In a blur of ecstasy, she turned to him, drawing him down and seeking his mouth with hers.

Wild. Free. Finally giving in.

She wanted to laugh or cry, maybe both, as they devoured each other, making up for lost time. She could hardly breathe as her hands glided down to his shoulders, his chest, wanting to feel the muscles that had developed over the years, the man she'd always hoped he'd grow into.

But it wasn't enough. None of it was, and he seemed to read that in her.

He brought a hand up to her breast—so achy, so in need of his touch.

Only his.

Only *him*.

They came up for air, his fingertips tracing her nipple, which pebbled against her bra and shirt.

"Dammit, Vi," he said, just before bending down to the other breast, slipping his hands behind her to press his mouth to the sensitized nub.

He sucked at her through the material, and she backed

against the counter, cradling his head, winding her fingers through his hair. A split of excitement bolted down the center of her, and it only got worse as he gently nipped at her, tonguing around her nipple until she moaned.

There was no anger in him now, only edged passion—the kind that makes a woman feel as if she was the only one he'd ever wanted.

Then he slowed down, kissing her breast, loving every curve, smoothing his hands to her backside and cupping her rear end. Bringing her closer.

She wrapped a leg around him, even as she heard something outside.

A car?

Through the puzzle pieces of her desire, she managed to look out the window. Her parents had arrived at the main house, grocery bags in hand, and they were checking out Davis's classic car.

"Wait," she said, pulling back from him.

Her heart was a flare, blazing and sparking until it pained her.

He'd spotted her parents outside the window, too, and after a moment's pause, he laughed.

She didn't understand at first, but then she caught on to the absurdity of their situation.

Teenagers once again. Nearly caught by her parents.

Some things never changed, even if the two of them had.

She ran her hands over Davis's thick hair, putting it back into place, then straightened his shirt. He watched her with a softness in his gaze that pierced her straight through.

"I guess it's time to go," he said.

"Looks that way."

He tucked a strand of her hair behind an ear. She bit her lip, not trusting herself.

But then he stepped away. "I'd say we've solved the whole 'friend' dilemma."

"Have we?"

He laughed again, going toward the door. "I'll see you later, Vi."

And, by his tone, she knew it wouldn't be as friends.

"I'm so happy you're here!" said Rita Niles, Violet's childhood friend, as they hugged.

It was late, and outside Rita's hotel, the volunteer cleanup crews were at work. Here, especially in the Old West tearoom, with its fringed curtains, velvet chairs, mahogany wood and flowered wallpaper, it was quiet. Most of the guests had checked out now that Founder's Weekend was over.

Rita's curly, long dark hair whisked against Violet's cheek as they pulled back from each other.

"Is Kristy up in your rooms?" Violet asked, wanting to say hi to Rita's little daughter.

"She's knocked out. We got back Friday night in time for Founder's Weekend, but it was a long trip, and you know how Kristy is whenever there's something going on in this town. It was impossible to get her to sleep with all the excitement."

"I'll see her tomorrow then. This'll give you and me a chance to talk."

"Sorry I didn't call you right when we got in…"

"As you said… Busy weekend."

Rita had already brought in tea service, and she poured the beverage into the rose-painted bone china cups from the matching pot. Tiny cucumber and sundried tomato sandwiches waited on plates, and Violet took one of them.

"You look tired, too," Rita said.

Violet finished munching on a sandwich, then said, "I got about three hours of sleep before I went in for my waitressing shift."

"I heard you won the dance marathon." Rita took a dainty sip of tea, her gray eyes glinting with interest.

"We did."

Rita set down her cup in its saucer. "We? As in you and Davis?"

Since there was no pulling the wool over Rita's eyes, Violet caught her up on everything that had happened since the last time they had talked—the emotional game of tag she'd been playing with Davis, the moment they'd caught up to each other when he'd taken her in his arms last night for the first slow dance.

Then this morning.

When Violet was done, Rita put down her cup. Violet tried to guess what her friend was thinking, but Rita was one of those people who'd always been very good at keeping her emotions under wraps. Maybe that was the reason they'd always gotten along.

"So your parents put the big kibosh on you and Davis this morning," Rita said.

"You could say that, but I'm not sure how far things would've gotten with him, anyway." Another lie. If it'd been up to her libido, they would've fallen into bed....

Violet shrugged off her confusion. "After Davis left, I went into the main house. My parents saw his car, so I figured I would do damage control before we got to work today."

"And?"

"I told them that Davis had dropped me off from the marathon and I gave him a little breakfast."

"Breakfast. That's a new way to say it."

Violet couldn't hold back a smile. Then she said, "Dad didn't have any comments the whole time."

"You said that something seemed to have changed with him last night, with Davis at the dance."

"Right."

"Maybe he saw two people who are nuts about each other, and he knows you're a big enough girl to make her own decisions about what she wants now."

The acknowledgment gnarled in Violet's tummy. Hearing someone besides her and Davis talk about their attraction made it more real.

"It'd be nice if Dad was ready to let bygones be bygones," Violet said. "But that doesn't mean he won't be all over Davis if something were to go wrong again."

"Like it did the first time?"

"Exactly. Also, there's the whole Mama Jackson problem. She read me the riot act last night, pretty much warning me to stay away from Davis."

"You told her to back off, of course."

"In so many words. But that didn't make it any easier."

Rita picked at her sandwich. "You and Davis always were affected by what both your parents thought of you. And, in your case, you cared too much about what *anyone* said, even if you pretended not to care."

"Well, family lasts forever. So do friends like you. But boyfriends…"

It seemed odd to dismiss Davis as something so insignificant.

Rita cocked her head sympathetically. "I wish I could give you advice, but you know how my love life has gone."

Five years ago, Rita's high-school sweetheart and fiancé had left her high and dry, pregnant with Kristy. Rita had recovered and raised a beautiful little girl, but not without a lot of sweat and tears.

Violet laid her hand over Rita's, which was resting on the table near her sandwich plate. "I'm not sure I need advice as much as a friendly ear."

"St. Val's isn't exactly full of those for either of us."

"For an arrogant miner's kid and the good girl who didn't want any meddling advice about how to single-handedly raise her child? No, it hasn't been, but believe it or not, things have gotten better since I've been back. I think people are seeing that I've got good intentions."

And she could thank Davis for some of that.

An employee stuck her head into the room. "Rita? Sorry to bother you, but can you come to the front desk for a second?"

Rita stood, brushing off her dark, knee-length uniform skirt, which went so well with the old-fashioned white top and its high collar. "I'll be back in a flash."

"I'll be here."

While Rita was gone, Violet sipped more tea. Her body—from head to toe—was tingling from the thought of Davis and how close they'd gotten to the edge this morning. He'd made it clear that they weren't going to be friends, and whether she could handle it or not, the temptation to find out exactly what he had in mind next made Violet wait in anticipation.

No matter how much her common sense told her to stay away.

Amati Street was deserted except for the men and women who were on their way home from tidying up the area and packing their artisan tents.

Davis had been one of those volunteers, and as he walked down the street, everything seemed stripped bare, without the bunting and laughter that had decorated St. Valentine hours ago.

But maybe the place seemed extra empty because Violet wasn't here.

Aaron Rhodes had his car keys dangling from his fingers as he passed Davis near the church, with its white picket fence and pristine paint job.

"Another year, another weekend," the other man said on his way by.

And not a very profitable one, at that. "See you around, Aaron."

The carpenter waved goodbye, and Davis continued down the street. Back to thinking about the Amati story, back to looking out for Jared Colton, whom he hadn't seen all weekend.

Back to thinking about Violet.

His head was still in the clouds, his body an adrenalized time bomb, set ticking from the time they'd spent together this morning.

But what now? How was he going to win over her heart?

He was still working that out when he passed his office on the way to the parking lot.

There was someone sitting on a nearby bench, half-shadowed but recognizable in her light-hued designer dress.

"Mom," he said. He hadn't seen her since last night, when she'd laid into Violet.

Under the glow of the gas lamps, he could see that she was holding an unlit cigarette. She'd been struggling to stay off them for years now, and whenever she thought of going back to it, this was the first step—holding it but not lighting up.

Her words came out in a tight rush. "I came back to apologize. I didn't intend to embarrass you last night, Davis. That confrontation shouldn't have happened in public."

"It shouldn't have happened at all." He felt a little sorry for her, sitting all alone. This was one of those times when he wondered if she was thinking of his father. The cigarettes usually came out when she got sentimental.

"It's hard to let go of what you've always believed or

felt," she said. "You, of all people, should understand that."

"Are you talking about how I'm holding on to Violet?"

She sighed. "I know I need to turn aside from your personal business. It's a bad habit of mine to get into it. But yes, I think Violet is a bad habit of *yours*."

"I thought you said you were going to stay out of it."

She lifted the cigarette to her mouth, then lowered it again, not answering.

"Mom," he said. "We've come a long way, and I don't want to lose ground on that. You're my mother, and I'll never have another one. But you can't ask me to give her up."

"She's a part of your past."

"So you've told me."

"And you were this damned stubborn the last time. After you two broke it off, you came to me, asked me what I'd done. I was honest with you about the lie I told her."

She'd added that Violet wasn't good enough, of course, but he'd come to suspect that no one would ever be good enough for her son. She was fine with his flings, but as soon as he'd gotten serious with someone…

"Do you think," he said, "that you can keep my heart from being broken like yours was when Dad died?"

She pushed the cigarette into her mouth, as if it would stop words from coming out.

He sighed, not knowing what else to say. But after a few seconds, she talked around the cigarette.

"Go. Do what you need to do with her. It'll be a hard lesson, but you'll eventually learn."

When he'd mentioned Dad, he'd hit a target. And, now, he supposed it was okay to let her avoid the subject. There were probably some things they'd never be honest with each other about, and this was one of them.

He held his hand out to her, and she looked up at him. Years of guarding herself were etched into her gaze.

"Let's get you to your car," he said.

When he had her safely behind the wheel, he watched her leave.

Then he took out his phone and dialed Violet's number, his heart skipping a beat when she answered.

"What are you doing tomorrow night?" he asked, smiling, his mother's warnings already a memory.

Chapter Nine

When Violet had accepted Davis's dinner invitation, she would've been comfortable with going out of town to the fish shack at Dempsy Lake or grabbing a quick bite at the Orbit Diner.

But this?

She sat at a linen-draped table on the dock that perched over the man-made lake in front of Davis's stone mansion. The amber lights from the windows gleamed off the rippling moonlit water, the slight wind flirting with the flames from the candles on the table.

Champagne waited in a bucket filled with ice as Davis took a seat across from her. At the last minute, he'd checked in with the staff in the so-called boathouse, which was really just another name for a gorgeous cottage overlooking the lake.

Violet straightened her sleek red dress, another cocktail number she'd tucked away in her closet, thinking she'd have no use for it in St. Valentine.

Little had *she* known.

"You shouldn't have gone through all this trouble," she said. Even if he'd just given her a peanut butter and jelly sandwich on a bench in town, she would've been as excited—and torn—to see him. Money had never mattered, only their time together, stolen and ultimately not meant to last.

"What, this is trouble?" he asked, pulling the champagne bottle out of the ice bucket. He'd tamed his dark blond hair, combing it back, and it made him look sharp—especially with the suit he was wearing.

"Don't act like this is no big deal, Davis," she said. "You flew in a private chef."

"She had the night off from the Houston hotel I invested in."

"She's been in charge of five-star restaurants."

"She makes food I like."

Davis popped the cork on the champagne. Some of it bubbled out and they laughed together. It felt so good to be laughing with him again, especially after she'd come to believe that there would be only bitterness while she was here.

He filled her flute, then his, and they raised their glasses for a toast.

"Here's to a sparkling future," he said. "For St. Valentine and for you."

"And you," she added.

For us?

As they drank, those unspoken words hovered between them.

There just couldn't be an *us*. Not unless Davis could understand that they would only be a temporary thing, and Violet doubted the possibility, what with their tempestuous history of getting in too deep and too fast, then self-destructing.

She took another sip. Then, not sure what to do next, she resorted to a neutral topic. "Since I had the day off from the saloon, I went to Rita's hotel to see if Jared Colton was there."

Davis put his glass on the table. If he was disappointed that they weren't taking up where they'd left off in her kitchen yesterday, he didn't show it. "Let me guess—our look-alike was out and about, riding around in his truck to Lord-knows-where."

"His truck was gone from the hotel's lot. When I asked Rita if he was still checked in, she wouldn't tell me. She's big on privacy, and even *I* can't play the friend card with her to squeeze out any information. But I wheedled the truth out of a new clerk who didn't know any better."

"So Jared's still in town."

"Sure is." Violet ran a finger down her flute. "The good news is that I talked to Jerry Lister today during my break." He was an old mining friend who still hung out with her dad. "He told me something that makes me think we've only hit the tip of the iceberg with Tony Amati."

Davis leaned forward, his voice even lower, sexier. "Yeah?"

Oh, yeah.

And…no. She shouldn't be *oh-yeah*ing about him. But why had she come here tonight if some part of her hadn't been willing to fall into his arms again?

She stilled her flailing heart. "Jerry remembers overhearing a conversation his father was having with a friend on the front porch when he was a kid. They were talking about Tony Amati and how there was some rumor about his 'mysterious origins.'"

"Even more mysterious than Tony is to us nowadays?"

"Definitely." Violet leaned forward, too, lowering her voice. Her skin felt as if waves of flickering awareness were traveling over it…and under it. "Everyone says that Tony used to be a Texas Ranger before he founded St. Valentine, but Jerry swears that he heard the man had some 'empty years.'"

"What does that mean?"

"I don't know, but Jerry's dad said something about Tony *having* to come back out West because of some trouble, as if Tony was running from something. Hiding in plain sight."

Davis put his hand over hers, squeezing it. "You did good, Vi."

He didn't remove his hand, and its warmth enveloped Violet.

Impetuously, she turned her hand over, wanting to feel his palm against hers. His flesh, manly and rough from the work he probably did on the ranch here, gave her a comfort she'd never felt before. And it brought back memories that made her quiver with sensation.

His hand on her hip, under her shirt, dragging up, up...

A young waiter dressed all in black came out of the cottage, bearing appetizer plates, and Violet let go of Davis.

He didn't look frustrated, though—he had a cocky glint in his blue eyes that reminded her of how he'd looked right after he'd kissed her for the first time in high school.

This is just the start, that look seemed to say.

After the waiter asked if they would like freshly ground pepper on their lobster Caesar salad, he left to bring them the wine that Davis had paired with their food—a light Chardonnay. After pouring it, he left them to their meal.

Water lapped at the dock. Violet used her fork to spear a bite of salad, her pulse pumping a mile a second.

Saved by the food. This time.

But how was she going to handle the rest of the night? Part of her still wanted to run from what she saw in Davis's gaze, but part of her needed him against her, inside her, just as it used to be.

Which part was right?

The silence was too much for her. "So you've got a pretty great life here."

"I like it just fine."

"Do you ever sail in this lake?"

"Not yet, but I wouldn't rule it out."

His voice was that low scratch over her skin that she fantasized about when she didn't have her defenses up and running.

Jeez, she was playing with fire, wasn't she? But she couldn't have stayed away from him, even if it was the best thing for her.

"If I were you," she said, "I'd own one of those little sailboats. A Sunfish."

"A one-man rig?"

"That's right." The "one-man" part had sounded louder than the rest of the words to her, and she wondered if she would always want a one-man—or one-woman—vessel.

All of a sudden, it sounded so lonely.

She continued. "Believe it or not, I didn't get to the ocean much in L.A., but when I did, I always dreamed of renting a Sunfish."

"I do some swimming here in the mornings. But mostly I ride or work in the stables."

"It must be nice to be rich enough to enjoy menial work."

"I'm not complaining." He grinned, almost devilishly. "You wouldn't, either."

A loaded comment, but she sidestepped it, even while the lure of this kind of life—of luxury, of nights having dinner with a private chef on the banks of your own lake—intrigued her.

If she had money, she would first get her parents out of their financial lurch. And, like Davis, she'd also do the same for her friends and community...

She stopped. *Her* community?

When had she started feeling as if St. Valentine were hers?

Davis finished off a hearty bite of salad. "If you didn't

go to the beach in L.A., what did you do with your extra time? Do you still read like you used to?"

"I wish, but there's no—"

"Time." Davis nodded. "You're busy."

When he said it, the words rang hollow. Busyness had somehow taken her over. Even back in St. Valentine, when she'd been running here and there because of the paper and school, she'd had time for kissing Davis, for looking into his eyes and getting lost in them.

From her purse on the dock, her phone sounded off—two dings signaling that she had a text message.

She ignored it, but Davis said, "Check it."

"Not during dinner with you."

"I don't mind."

But she wouldn't do it. Davis had taken a lot of care with dinner tonight, and this was his time. Even if it wasn't wise to give him her heart, she could sure give him...

Well, her attention, right?

Soon, the main course arrived—grilled lamb loin with black olives, artichokes, potatoes and a tomato confit—and they continued with their small talk: more about the sort of stories she'd written on the city beat, more about Davis's extensive list of properties, including a golf course near Dallas and a resort near El Paso.

The meal ended with a warm cherry and chocolate cobbler, and soon afterward Violet was holding her stomach as she thanked and complimented Chef Hartford.

And then she and Davis strolled away from the dock and toward his home.

Her mind raced along with her blood. What would happen next?

What did she *want* to happen?

They came to stand in front of the sliding glass doors of his home—windows into the scary, enticing world inside. Low light burned from the rustic yet elegant chandeliers, echoing the glow inside of her.

Davis rested his hands on her shoulders—his fingers on the bare skin left exposed by her dress. She went shivery all over.

"All night," he said, "I've been across that table from you. I kept looking at you, Vi, thinking how beautiful you look—how beautiful you always look, whether it's in this dress or just every day. And I asked myself how I wanted to handle this."

This—the moment in which they'd have to decide where to go from here.

Her voice was breathy. "What conclusion did you come to?"

He reached up, running his knuckles over her cheek. Just a simple touch like that was enough to turn her into water, simmering and near to boiling.

"Slow," he said, and that was all.

But it was definitive, making her think of slow kisses, a slow hand caressing her face, then skimming down and over her collarbone, coming to her breast.

Her body reacted, her nipples going hard, even at the mere thought.

"How slow?" she asked.

"As slow as you need for it to be."

A breath escaped her, and she realized she'd been

holding it. "Davis, I don't know what I could possibly bring to your life that you don't already have."

He frowned.

How could she avoid angering him if she admitted that she was afraid he was just going to get tired of her once he'd had his fun? How could she tell him that getting back together with him was terrifying to her because she couldn't take it if their relationship soured again?

He whispered, "You really don't know what you do for me?"

"I know what I did do. You used to say that I made you feel smarter than anyone had ever given you credit for. I used to make you see yourself in a whole different way—a good way."

"And you still do."

"No, you did all that yourself after I left. You became your own person."

"Because of you."

This was too much. She'd never expected that his feelings for her would've stayed alive…and that hers would still be the same ones, too, if she would only allow them free reign.

He stroked her cheek. "I'll wait, Vi, just as long as I have to. Know that."

Her practical side shouted that they didn't have all the time in the world—she'd be gone just as soon as she could be, and where would that leave them? Hurt and angry again?

He must have seen her confusion, because he bent to

her, gathering her in his arms and bringing her against him as his mouth sought hers.

Slow, sipping, he tasted her lips as if she was a fine champagne he had been saving for the right occasion.

When he finished, it felt as if she was steeped in thick liquid, making it difficult—and yet so easy—to think that everything could work out.

She rested her mouth against his chest, and he whispered into her hair.

"Will you see me tomorrow?"

The old Violet would've told him that she had more interviews planned before her late shift at the bar and grill.

"Yes," she said. *God, yes.*

He gave her one more kiss—gentle and filled with promise—before he clasped her hand in his and walked her to a town car that would take her back home.

A final kiss, and he eased her into the backseat, standing there in the moonlight for one more moment, his gaze devouring her.

He shut the door, and the driver took off down the lane that led to the country road that would bring her home to a bed that would feel all too empty tonight.

Blowing out a breath, she remembered the text that had come through during dinner, then took her phone out of her purse.

The message was from her L.A. friend Nancy, and when Violet focused on the content, she sat forward in her seat.

Might be an opening in San Fran for you!
Call you soon if I hear anything else.

Violet shoved the phone back into her purse and looked out the window, back toward Davis's place, when it probably would've been a better idea to be looking ahead.

Davis called Violet the next morning.

"Be ready for me to pick you up in an hour," he said on the phone, as he put a cooler in the backseat of another one of his restored cars—a 1947 black Mercury convertible.

"Where are we going?" she asked.

He climbed in. "I can't tell you, but dress comfortably, like you're going to be outside."

"Shorts? Skirts? What?"

"I like you in anything." *Or out of anything,* he silently added with a grin, signing off by telling her he'd see her soon.

When he drove up to her cabin on the Osbornes' ranch, she came outside as if she'd been watching for him through the window.

As he got out to hold open her door, he couldn't take his eyes off her. She wore a floral sleeveless top that knotted at her waist and khaki shorts that cupped her rear end, making his fantasies go wild. She'd pulled her hair back into a high ponytail, leaving her neck bare.

Her neck—delicate, pale, gorgeous. Just made for the kisses he was going to give her.

For some reason, her smile wasn't as bright as it'd been last night, when she'd gone home from their dinner. But then, as if he'd merely imagined it, she smiled brightly, nearly knocking him out.

"So what's it going to be?" she asked, peering into the backseat at the blanket and cooler. "A picnic? Did I wear the right shoes for where we're going?" She showed him her cute, strappy sandals.

"Perfect," he assured her, meaning it in more than one way. She was perfect, after all.

He put pedal to the metal. Then, after driving for about twenty minutes out of the St. Valentine town limits, he pulled into a dirt lane that brought them to an old ranch with a red-paint-patched barn and a corral. A withered cabin that had seen better days eyed them with broken windows.

As Violet got out of the car, she shot him a curious glance. "What's this about?"

"It's some property I invested in recently."

"Looks like this one's going to need some work." She smiled and wandered over to the cabin, where some purple flowers were growing.

"It's an investment, all right," he said quietly, watching her.

Then, as she picked the flowers, he grabbed the cooler, a bag of food he'd purchased from the market and a blanket from the back of the car, and made his way toward the corral. The summer sun beat down, but there was a lean-to.

He spread the blanket on the ground, sat, then brought out a couple of wineglasses for the champagne and orange juice in the cooler. She came over, skimming the flowers over his temple.

He grabbed her wrist and she laughed, sitting next to him and presenting him with a loose bouquet.

"Thanks," he said. He'd never gotten flowers from a woman in his life.

"Just a small token of my appreciation. Next time, I'm going to get the food, okay? You're doing too much for me."

As she moved away from him to fetch some plates, he once again thought of how hard to get, hard to hold, she was.

She's a part of your past, he heard his mom say.

"So why'd you buy this property?" Violet asked as she set out the paper plates.

He wasn't going to think of warnings today. "Always full of questions, aren't you?"

"Hey, I am who I am." When she smiled, the gesture seemed to die a little on her lips, as if she was remembering something, too. But then she recovered.

It almost made him think that he was being a stubborn fool, courting her like this. But he wanted to savor the buildup with Violet, show her how he felt before hopping into the sack with her, as he would've done with any other woman.

She was different.

She was the one for him, whether she knew it or not yet.

"I bought this place," he finally said, "because it has potential."

"For...?"

"You know me. I've got a lot of toys. The possibility for entertainment is endless with this."

She cocked an eyebrow as she stood, going to a section of corral fencing that was covered by the lean-to's shade. Glancing around, she seemed puzzled.

"I'm not seeing anything spectacular here, Davis."

"You always manage to in the end."

"Meaning…?"

They were at the point he'd been trying to reach— he'd brought her out here for a picnic, sure, but he also knew what Violet needed.

Restored confidence. The kind of pride that she'd brought out in him since she'd come back.

"You're the smartest woman I know," he said, "and I wanted your opinion on something."

She leaned against the fencing, hooked by this little mystery he was throwing out to her.

"It seems to me," he said, "that for St. Valentine to recover properly, it should start depending on itself for jobs. Not just on corporations or any outside influences."

"You want to provide some opportunities here?"

"Yeah." He'd known it wouldn't take long for her to figure it out. "We've already talked about how to draw people to St. Valentine, and this could be another way. I was thinking of having some sort of operating ranch here—one that benefits all kinds of people through the Helping Hand Foundation. Something that could employ locals."

It was as if he'd lit her up. "Ooo—like a ranch for kids to raise horses? Once I did a story about a place near L.A. that hosts so-called directionless children who need somewhere to go so they can learn how to be responsible. Animals are good therapy for them. So is having a job when they're out of school, and Lord knows enough of *those* aren't available around here."

He might've been one of those kids if Violet hadn't come along and shown him that there was more to him than a social scoundrel.

Her gaze was shiny as she looked at him. *In*to him, it seemed.

"Davis," she said, "you're a surprise a minute."

"It's nothing." He shrugged. "It's only an idea."

"One of many." She bit her lip, glancing around, maybe even seeing what he saw in this place now. "You know what's great? If something had happened and you didn't have all your money, you would've been a success, anyway. You could've done anything you wanted to do."

For a man who'd feared that everyone in St. Valentine thought he was nothing more than a rich boy, that was a balm.

"I'm a lot like you then," he said quietly. "You can do anything, too."

She hesitated. "These days, I feel like I don't have much choice in the matter."

He hated to see her sad, and he stood, taking a step toward her—near enough to put his hands on her arms, sparking the electricity between them. "You'll always have a choice."

He meant himself. She should choose *him*, whether it seemed like a crazy idea or not.

When she looked him in the eye, he saw hesitation there. "Davis, last night..."

"Was a start."

She seemed anguished. "Last night was wonderful, in so many ways. But that text I got during dinner?"

She's a part of your past....

He pushed the warning aside again. "What did it say?"

Her words were thick. "There might be a position opening on a paper in San Francisco. My friend has inside word about it, and..."

He let go of her arms as the past wound around him, repeating itself.

Violet leaving town again. His heart cracking into pieces that he'd never quite picked up until she'd come back.

Last time, he'd let her go without a fight, but this time...

Hell, no.

He kissed her with such passion—and possession—that she made a soft noise against his mouth. And as the kiss deepened, their desire grew frenzied, breathless.

After getting lost in the seemingly endless moments, he trailed his mouth up her jaw, pressing his lips against her ear. "Are you going to tell me you don't feel anything after that?"

Hazily, she looked into his eyes, and he saw the maelstrom of emotion.

"I just don't want anyone to get hurt," she said.

"Why would it have to turn out that way?"

"Because—"

He cut off the same old arguments by kissing her again. Now, though, it seemed as if she'd thrown away every excuse she'd been clinging to, and she leaned back against the fence, pulling him with her until the wood creaked under their weight.

But it held strong as she pressed against him, pulling him down so they were chest to chest, hip to hip.

"Vi," he whispered, "you're not going *anywhere*."

She didn't contradict him, only tugged at his shirt in an effort to unbutton it. He fumbled right along with her until she delved her hands under the gaping material, palms against his ribs, exploring as if he was new territory.

And, in a way, he was. Being with her again wouldn't be like the last time—there were too many years gone by, too many experiences they couldn't ignore.

He loosened her ponytail, and her hair rained over his hands. Captured by the scent of her, he picked her up, making his way back to the convertible, where there was a long, upholstered backseat.

Just like the one they'd made love on the first time.

He got the back door open, and he laid her down, her hair red-kissed and enticing against the white vinyl.

"My Violet," he said under his breath, as he climbed in.

Slow, though. He'd told himself this would go slow, that he would revel in every moment with her, stretching it out until she couldn't tell the difference between now and forever.

He slid his hands up her hips, her waist, making her hold her breath as he stroked over her ribs. His thumbs caught her sensitized nipples and he circled them, bringing her to even harder peaks through her thin top.

She ran her hands up and down his arms, watching

him, something like fear mixed with utter ecstasy in her light brown gaze.

He thought of how she would look without all these clothes, and he could barely stand the wait to find out how different she would be. But he forced himself to undo the buttons on her top in an unhurried rhythm, one, another, until he got down to where the material tied into a knot.

Just as he had done with those ribbons in the box on Founder's Weekend, he untangled the knot, taking off her top until her pale skin greeted him, the lace of her bra the only thing between him and her breasts.

When he reached behind her to unclasp her bra, she arched, sending her hips against him, and he sucked in a breath.

"Hurry," she said, restless.

Not on his life.

He slid one bra strap down, guiding her hand through the strap. He did the same with the other, then deliberately pulled at the bra until it was off.

His core hummed as he looked at her breasts, definitely more womanly now, full and shapely even when she was lying down. The pink tips were hard and he came forward, latching his mouth to one.

She rocked against him again, and he eased his hands to her back, bringing her to him.

Damn, she tasted as good as she smelled—cherries and almonds and musk, and a bit of summer sweat. He tugged on her nipple, playing with it, and she made bothered little sounds.

He kissed her breast, then cupped her rear end, positioning himself so that her groin was grinding against his.

Already hard and ready—but he was going slow.

As slow as it took to show her that she was meant to stay in this town.

And with him.

Chapter Ten

Was this what it had been like before with Davis?

When they'd been summer lovers fifteen years ago, had she felt as if her heart were about to burst, right along with every other part of her body? Had there been such devastating, sizzling currents blasting through her, threatening to burn her alive from the inside out?

Now, as he rubbed against her, torturing her until a cry bubbled in her lungs, Violet couldn't believe she had ever felt this blissful—couldn't believe that anyone on earth had.

Sensation took over as he undid the front of her shorts, then smoothed a hand into her panties.

A rough, needful sound escaped her when his finger slipped between her folds.

He drew his finger up, down, up again, circling the

achiest part of her, pressing down on it until she strained against him.

She wanted all of him now. He'd been right—she *didn't* want to leave town again.

Didn't want to leave him.

Flashes of what could've been—no, what *could be*—took her over—days and nights of languid affection as bedsheets wrapped around them, binding them to each other. Hours in his arms as they listened to the grass near his lake rustling in a breeze as the seasons changed.

All of it filled her up in a way she'd never, ever expected...

He glided a finger inside her, and she grabbed at his loose shirt.

"Davis..."

The pleasure in his gaze was a potent aphrodisiac, more powerful than any expensive champagne he could buy. He slipped his finger in, out, bringing her to a restless brink.

Slow, she thought. He'd wanted them to go slow.

Forget slow.

She tore at his shirt, yanking it off him, and he helped her. But when she made herself stop for a second, just to put her hand over his heart, just to feel it pistoning as much as hers was, he paused, too.

He grasped her hand, raising it to his face, pressing it there, then turning his lips to her palm to kiss it.

It was almost like a pledge of sorts—a wordless vow that things would be different this time around, that nothing truly would ever stand in their way.

You thought the same thing last time...

She shut her eyes against the voice of reason, because this wasn't reasonable at all—what she was feeling, what she was willing to leave behind in her "other" life, now that she and Davis were together.

But why be reasonable when that was just about all she had been before in life? Wasn't it time to let herself go?

She touched Davis's face with her fingertips as he still held her hand. Then he released her, and she stroked downward, over his strong chest, down the center of his hard abs, until she got to the trail of downy hair that disappeared into the waistband of his jeans.

No stopping now...

And she didn't. Wouldn't.

She eased her hand down, over the bulge in his jeans, and he hauled in a sharp breath. Then she traced her thumb over the outline of his tip.

"It's time," she said.

In answer, he smoothed the hair back from her forehead, taking her in with a heart-banging gaze, escalating her pulse to an agonizing rhythm that echoed low in her belly. Then he tugged down her shorts and panties, bringing her sandals along with them.

He spread her legs slightly, and the vulnerability she should've felt never materialized.

"Dammit, Violet," he whispered, looking at her, turning her on that much more just before he took off the rest of his clothing.

He grabbed a packet from a jeans pocket, then discarded them altogether.

"Let me," she said. She'd never been this bold with him before.

She freed the condom and sheathed him with it. This was it—no turning back. And right now, that didn't scare her. It invigorated her as she pulled him down to her.

As if retaliating, he teased her with his erection, then finally entered her with one smooth thrust.

The world went misty for Violet—a bank of damp, white fog that clung to her skin as she floated through it. The air undulated, caressing her skin, the lining of her tummy—everything as it pulled her along, growing thicker and thicker.

As she moved with Davis's every motion, she felt as if the mist was reaching into her, raising her, turning her every which way until she got so dizzy she didn't know which direction was up, which was down...

Tearing her apart...

Putting her back together again...

Apart—together—

The mist seemed to implode, vacuuming into her, then exploding outward instead, taking her with it.

Then, little by little, it dissipated, molecule by molecule...

Memory by memory...

Until it all coalesced into a moment in which she held on to Davis, unwilling to let him go.

They'd gotten through the fog.

And she was finally in his arms where there was no doubt anymore that she belonged.

There'd never even been a picnic that morning at the abandoned ranch.

Instead, Davis had driven Violet back to his home straightaway, a palpitating silence in the car. He'd kept one hand on the steering wheel and the other on her, as they held hands.

But, once through his doorway, they'd grasped at each other again, stumbling through the foyer and up the stairway to his room, where he closed the door and took her to his bed.

Now, some time later, after hours of enjoying each other in that bed, Davis was in the kitchen. He'd made sure Lloyd was busy outside the mansion, and that the maid had the rest of the afternoon off. He wanted Violet to have the run of his house, just as much as she had had the run of him.

His body was alive with her touch, his skin keening for her.

The entire time, he couldn't wipe a smile from his face. *She changed her mind about me,* he kept thinking, and it felt surreal, a fantasy.

But those other voices were whispering to him, too.

Part of your past...

What if she changes her mind again?

The niggles remained as he heard footsteps on the stairway, then on his carpet, and he turned toward the entry.

As Violet entered the kitchen, his belly clutched at the sight of her—she'd donned one of his long-sleeved shirts, and the hem hung down to midthigh. She was slender, but she'd always been that way, mostly because she burned off so many calories running around like a hellion with a million things on her to-do lists.

But she was all woman these days—sexy as hell, her

hair tossed about. When she saw him standing there with just his jeans on, her gaze lingered on his bare chest.

He didn't know how long he'd be able to stay on the other side of the room.

"Hey, there," she said.

"I thought you were never coming down."

"I had to do it sometime." She had a shift to work at her family's restaurant.

He wanted to offer her enough money to make sure her parents never had to worry about meeting payroll or keeping the saloon running, but the Osbornes would never accept that. He knew it from past experience with her dad.

And with Violet. Unlike most women, she seemed pretty unimpressed with, although still grateful for, him spending money on her.

She wandered closer to him, and he caught her scent. She smelled like him now, too, wearing his shirt.

Still wearing *him*.

Leaning against the counter nearby, she tucked her hands inside the long sleeves. "What a morning."

"I never did get to serve you brunch."

"I didn't notice."

They smiled as he opened the fridge, preparing to coddle her with food.

"Whoa," she said, slipping under his arm and popping up in front of him. She gave him a playful nudge back. "I told you—next time I'll be in charge of the meal."

He raised his hands in mock surrender. "I won't stand in your way."

She smirked, then got busy inspecting the contents of

his fridge. She brought out eggs, chives, a green and red pepper, cheddar and Monterey cheeses and butter. Then she plucked garlic salt and pepper from the spice rack.

"I thought you didn't cook," he said, crossing his arms over his chest, ready to be entertained.

"I don't go out of my way to do it. I hope you don't mind, but the only go-to recipe I really know offhand is how to make an egg scramble. It's hard to mess that up." She grinned back at him. "What, are you thinking of banishing me from your kitchen because I'm serving breakfast food after noon?"

"Nah, I'd kind of like to keep you around. You wear my shirts well."

She laughed, fetching cut-crystal glasses from one of his cupboards, completely at home in his kitchen.

He liked watching her move—unhooking a pan from where it was hanging over his kitchen island, pouring them both some carbonated, lemon-flavored water.

The scene seemed so right that he was almost surprised when she brought up a topic that neither of them had talked about yet.

"So," she said. "About that job in San Francisco I started to tell you about."

God, couldn't they just skip over this for the time being?

She commandeered a cutting board. After washing the vegetables, she began to chop them. "I was thinking of how I wouldn't know anyone there. It would be just like starting from scratch in a new job, new place."

What was she saying? "I thought that always seemed like an adventure to you."

"I was younger then." She hesitated, a lock of hair hiding her face.

Was she hinting about…staying?

A snap of fear blindsided him, and that took him aback.

Hadn't he been the one pursuing *her?* So why did he all of a sudden want to avoid the subject?

He grasped a reason that this might be freaking him out a little. This was where the fantasy would detach from reality for them, and what had Violet been to him most of his life except for a fantasy?

Slow, he thought. *Maybe we should drop the subject and still take it slow, not making any life decisions just yet.*

But why was he even thinking that when he'd been so sure about him and Violet before?

What if she changes her mind about us?

His head swam with confusion as she quietly added, "Maybe I could get used to newspaper stories about cats stuck in trees and the occasional big opportunity, like the story about Tony Amati. Maybe getting used to St. Valentine would be a big adventure in itself."

She said it as if she'd be happy with that. But a sinking feeling told him that she was lying to herself. She would get bored, then…

She would leave again.

Violet glanced back at him, as if waiting for him to confirm something. Anything.

But he wasn't doing it.

Slow…

She still might change her mind about us…

Now that she was in his kitchen, watching him to see why he was so silent, it was all too damned real.

Not knowing what else to do, he went to her, then kissed her on the forehead.

She seemed mildly bewildered, but then he realized just what to do to smooth things over until he could think some more.

"I've got something for you," he said.

He went to his study, where the whittled flower he'd bought from the ex-miners at Founder's Weekend was sitting. When he came back out, she was sautéing the vegetables. He waited until she'd taken them off the burner, then came up behind her.

He pressed the flower into her hand, and she looked down at it.

"You gave me flowers today," he said, "so I owed you one."

If she was ticked off that he was dancing around the serious subjects, she didn't mention it. "Where did you get this?"

He told her about the miners, even though he left out everything they'd said about her dad and her.

She smiled, running her finger over the etched petals. "It's beautiful."

Then she launched herself into his arms in a hug that made him feel like crap for even thinking she was going to break him again in the end.

His emotions had been on high after this morning, he told himself. That was all it was. And with the happiness and ecstasy there'd been room for some fear to sneak in.

They were going to be just fine.

He even kept thinking that as the edges of the whittled flower dug into his back while she hugged him, reminding him for an instant of another day long ago when he'd felt stabbed there by the same girl who was in his arms now.

Before Violet left that day, she and Davis had made plans to meet again the next night, after she had worked a morning shift at the restaurant then taken care of another old-timer interview.

As with most of the other interviews, this one didn't pan out much, except for more vivid anecdotes about St. Valentine, although not about Tony Amati himself.

But she was still feeling good about life. How could she not when she was with Davis?

As the sun curved down in the sky through her bedroom window, she wiggled into a light pink cocktail dress with a delicate silver netting draped over it. Yup, she was the happiest girl in the world. Sure, when she'd talked to Davis about the possible job in San Francisco yesterday, she'd expected more of a reaction out of him, but maybe her hints about staying in town had gone over his head. Maybe she needed to smack him with a clear-cut promise to stay in St. Valentine, even if she was offered a good job somewhere else.

But something in her wanted to be sure that she was making the right choice before she nixed a position on a paper that would help her career. Most of all, though, she wanted to hear him say *I love you.*

Should she just say it first?

She wondered if Davis's way of saying it had been

with that flower, which even now sat on her vanity table, looking as if it was just starting to bloom.

Surely everything would work out. There was nothing to worry about, even if anxiety nipped at her whenever she thought about turning down a great opportunity like the one in San Francisco…

Fifteen minutes later, she heard a car pull into the driveway. It wasn't the town car Davis had sent in the past but a limousine.

Davis got out of the backseat dressed in a suave gray suit that made him seem as if he'd just stepped out of a magazine ad.

She held her breath as he came to her door, then knocked. After brushing a hand down her dress and touching her upswept hair, just to make sure nothing was out of place, she went to him.

The moment she opened the door, she could tell that he'd been expecting her to look nice…but she'd surpassed even his imagination.

His gaze swept her from head to toe, leaving a thrill behind.

"You look just like a mermaid," he said.

She touched the silver netting on her dress. "Thank you?"

"It's a good thing. Guys have mermaid fantasies right along with French maids and Catwoman."

Glowing with the compliment, she grabbed her handbag.

But he had something else for her. He held out a hand. A necklace with a diamond pendant dangled from it.

"I thought you might like this," he said, and waited

for her to turn around so he could fasten it around her neck. "I was in Houston for business and I saw it in a window."

While he was doing that, she thanked him. Yet, at the same time, she felt a little bit like he was adding a finishing touch to her—as if she wasn't quite complete in his eyes without it.

But that was silly.

When she turned back around, he touched the pendant, smiled in approval, then grabbed her hand and led her to the limo.

The interior was dimly lit, with tiny lights stretched along the floorboards, mirrored wood and a minibar. Although there were two long seats that faced each other, he sat next to her.

"A girl could get spoiled with you," she said.

"I like to make you happy, Vi."

And he did just that. Made her very happy.

As they drove, he poured her a glass of Sauternes that had been chilling. "I thought we'd have cocktails in here."

She knew they were going to Houston's Historic District, to a French restaurant he had a financial stake in. Chevalier, it was called, and from what she'd read about it, it was expensive and elegant.

The trip lasted under an hour while they drank their wine, and by the time they arrived, Violet was slightly buzzed. She didn't think it was because of the alcohol— she was pretty sure Davis just did that to her.

He helped her out of the limo, and out of pure instinct

she stood on her tiptoes and kissed him, long and yearningly.

After yesterday, she was assuming this was the first night of the rest of their lives, and there was something frightening and wonderful about that.

An adventure.

He brought her inside the marbled lobby, which was charmingly decorated with crystal chandeliers, tasteful boudoir furniture and original Degas art. Then they headed to the private elevator that would take them to the roof.

When they arrived, Violet saw that there was only one table overlooking the city lights, as well as a lone violin player and a server who'd been waiting for them.

"Where's the restaurant?" Violet asked.

"It's downstairs, but we'll consider this our private dining room."

It just got better from there. He treated her to a decadent meal, and she reveled in every course—the diver sea scallops they started off with, the classic Dover sole prepared tableside and the chocolate soufflé.

She was wondering, though, if they would ever get around to sorting out their future. She tried once to bring it up, but Davis seemed intent on providing them with a fun night.

"There's plenty of time to sort things out later," he said, and she believed him.

Was she the one who was already taking things too fast?

Had she been doing too much assuming that he would want to just jump right into a serious relationship?

Her inner skeptic reminded her that he had never said he had loved her since she'd returned, and it remembered what their first kiss as adults had been like—angry, in need of her body.

Had he gotten what he needed from her then? Was he already becoming bored of the woman who'd gotten away—the one he'd recently caught again?

But then why was he still courting her?

By the time they'd finished their meal, Davis had even more in store for her.

"Are you ready?" he asked, looking as excited as a kid with a bunch of unwrapped presents in front of him.

"Davis," she said, "I don't know what you have planned, but this was more than enough." What would it take for him to see that all these trappings didn't mean as much to her as just being with him did?

"You'll change your mind about that in a second," he said.

And they were off, heading down in that private elevator again. Except, when it landed on the ground floor, he didn't usher her into the limo. He brought her out of the lobby and off into a hallway lined with ultra-chic stores.

He guided her into one, which was decorated in tones of deep red and velvet. "Clair de Lune" played over the speakers. A model-thin woman with patrician features and spun-gold hair wound into a high, braided bun stood by the entrance, her hands folded in front of her.

"Good evening, Mr. Jackson."

"Evening, Norah."

The woman inspected Violet, as if she were taking her measurements, then she smiled.

"I'm looking forward to this, Miss Osborne."

"What?" Violet asked, although she suspected what Davis might have in mind.

He sat on a plush loveseat. "You said you didn't have many fancy dresses, so I thought we should take care of that since you're going to have need of them."

Violet's girlish side gave a little leap. Shopping. Who didn't love that?

But there was something about the situation that made her feel…kept. Indulged, in some way, as if Davis were compensating for something else.

As if he weren't sure how a relationship was supposed to go.

But she had to be wrong about that.

Norah brought her into a back room that was veiled with blushing, sheer material next to long mirrors. On the side, there was an entire rack of mouth-watering, sigh-inducing dresses in Violet's favorite colors.

The shopkeeper took one, a mossy green number that would drape over a woman's body and make her look like a Grecian goddess.

Violet allowed the woman to hold the dress against her. "How did you know what sizes I take? And what colors to choose?"

"Mr. Jackson sent me your information and a description of your coloring."

Sneaky. He must've caught a glimpse of her clothes tags yesterday when she'd had them off.

"If I don't say so myself," Norah added, "I did rather

well." She smiled. "You're going to stun him. Not that you don't already. You must be special for him to do this for you."

The words sighed through Violet. *Special.*

Yes, he did make her feel that way, even without a shopping spree.

To think, she'd gone halfway across the country to find a specialness within her someplace else when, all along, she'd had it in St. Valentine, with Davis.

Norah left her alone to undress then garb herself in the mossy creation. The fabric moved over her body like water. Violet hardly even recognized herself, and although it made her feel like a princess, it also made her feel...

As if it wasn't her in the mirror.

When she returned, Norah nodded with satisfaction. "Now we show Mr. Jackson."

Suddenly, Violet felt a shyness creep up on her. Odd, because only yesterday she and Davis had been as intimate as two people could be.

She went back into the showroom, and the second she stepped through the curtains, Davis rose to his feet.

He didn't have to say anything—his gaze spoke volumes about wanting and needing, about what he would do to her if he had her alone.

But was that enough anymore?

Should she say what should be said next and commit herself based on one day of passion?

As he walked over to her, Norah conveniently disappeared.

"You take my breath away, Violet," he whispered.

And your heart, too?

She kept asking herself this the rest of the night, as she tried on more dresses for him, as he took her up to the finest room in the hotel—a suite with a hot tub and a massive bed fitted with white satin sheets that had rose petals strewn over the covers.

It was heaven in so many ways, but in the morning, after they'd driven back to St. Valentine, she got the call.

And that was when everything changed, whether they were ready or not.

Chapter Eleven

"The editor of the *Chronicle* wants you to interview for a staff writing position?" Rita asked after Violet told her the news that early afternoon. "In San Francisco?"

"That's what he said." They were upstairs in Rita's hotel, in a suite that served as her and her daughter Kristy's quarters. Like the rest of the place, there was an Old West feel—Victorian-style furniture and antiques, lots of velvet and gilded mirrors.

From an adjoining room, the sounds of a cartoon escaped as little Kristy enjoyed her entertainment. Davis had dropped Violet off early just so she could get ready at her cabin, then fulfill a babysitting promise she'd made to Rita.

She'd gotten the call from the *Chronicle* editor right after stepping out of the shower. "We had a really good phone interview," Violet said, her pulse dragging. "He wants me to fly out there this week for a second one."

Rita stood by the door. She'd just been about to run the errands she'd been putting off during her trip out of town. "What about...?"

"I haven't told Davis yet."

She didn't ever want to tell him. What she *wanted* to do was magically know just how he was feeling about her, aside from all the candlelight dinners and dress shopping. She wanted to be able to call up the editor and tell him that she was off the market because she would never leave Davis.

But was it too early for that? How did Davis really feel?

And what was really between them?

"Vi," Rita said. "What are you going to do?"

She shook her head. "I've got to tell him. Then I'll see how he reacts."

"Isn't it obvious how he's going to react?"

If only it were that easy. Ever since she and Davis had made love the other day, something about him had been...different. And she knew that she should've asked him why, but it was hard for her to think of what he might say.

I had you, and I'm ready to move on... Or, *It was great, Vi, but my mom was right. I'm never going to settle down. Being with you just confirmed that.*

But she just couldn't sit here thinking that way. She had to suck it up and straighten out whatever was going on with them, because thanks to Davis she knew exactly where she wanted to be now.

By his side.

It had taken one night back in his arms to drive that point home.

Rita hugged Violet goodbye, then departed with a sympathetic glance. But surely everything would go all right with Davis when Violet told him about the interview, and how she'd been tempted by the opportunity but she wasn't going to take it if he could offer a reason for her to stay here in St. Valentine.

When she broached the subject again, would he give her more than a whittled wooden flower this time?

She dug into her purse, bringing out a ribbon that she used to loosely tie back her hair. Then she went into the family room, where Kristy was watching some kind of cartoon with a goofy fairy and her minions. Rita had told Violet that Kristy was under the weather today, although she didn't have a fever. Nonetheless, the child was in her Dora the Explorer pajamas, her curly dark hair making her look like a teeny version of her mother.

"Hey," Violet said. "How are you feeling?"

"Sleepy."

She sat on the overstuffed couch, and Kristy leaned her head against her. Touched, Violet slid her arm around the girl and sank down in her seat.

For four years, Violet had sent Kristy cards every holiday and birthday, just like an aunt would. Actually, Rita had named Violet an honorary aunt, and even during her infrequent, brief visits to St. Valentine, it would take Kristy only about fifteen minutes to fully warm up to Violet again.

She thinks you're the best, Rita would joke every time.

Now, as Kristy drifted off to sleep, a warmth drifted around in Violet's chest, settling in the center of it.

What would it be like to have a daughter?

Davis's child?

Heat pricked her throat. She'd always assumed that love meant having a family, but even though she'd been intimate with Davis, even though he'd been her first love, how well did she really know him?

How much had they talked these things through before hopping in the sack together?

She thought of how he'd given her that diamond pendant necklace and those dresses last night, making her over into a far fancier version of what she actually was. Then she thought of how he had wanted their relationship to stay under the radar all those years ago.

Why did it feel as if he was keeping her a bit under the radar once again, guiding her out of her waitressing outfits or off-the-rack clothing, making her over into a society girl, the sort of woman Davis Jackson was expected to take to his social events and business dinners?

To think, she'd spent a lot of effort in erasing the miner's daughter from her, bettering herself, and it was almost as if Davis wanted that, too—but even more so. It stung that she still might not be enough for him.

That train of thought hounded her as Kristy slept on, as Violet watched that silly fairy on the TV changing a girl frog into a princess.

When she heard someone knock on the front door, she went to answer it.

Davis stepped into the family room, and, for a moment, neither of them said anything as a powerful rush of feeling swamped her.

Gradually, though, the sound of the TV came back to her, and she thought of Kristy in the next room. Violet smiled at Davis, then lifted a finger to her lips as she went back to the little girl and covered her with an afghan that was draped over the back of the couch.

When she looked back up, she saw Davis watching her and Kristy.

Was he moved in some way? Did he like seeing her with a child, and was he imagining that they were his own family?

Or maybe that was all in her head and she'd done what she'd told herself not to do, ever.

Fallen too hard and fast again.

With him.

Knowing she would never find out what was going on unless they actually had a heart-to-heart, she tucked a pillow under the child's head.

A little angel, she thought for the first time in her life, that warmth still suffusing her at the idea of a daughter—or a son—of her own.

Trying not to let her emotions run away from her, she passed Davis in the entryway, then pulled shut the door behind her as they stood in the front room.

He reached out to grasp the hem of her blouse, kissing her in a quiet hello. "I thought I'd drop by to say hi."

She smiled again, but he had that flirty grin on his face, and she almost hated to wipe it off with an unpleasant subject.

Then he extracted a creamy envelope from his inside jacket pocket and gave it to her.

"What's this?" she asked.

"Information about your free-for-all at a day spa in Houston. There's a personal shopper there who's waiting to take you on another spree, and you've got an appointment in the salon and also a massage...." He must've read the look on her face, because he trailed off. "What's wrong?"

A makeover.

"Davis," she said, "I told you, it's too much."

"I'd spend all I have on you. You know that."

"I'm not just talking about money or gifts."

Gradually, she saw the understanding cloud his eyes, and she knew that the time for fun had ended.

When Davis had spied Violet with Rita Niles's little girl, he'd been thunderstruck with an emotion he was hard-pressed to identify, even now.

Seeing Violet with the girl had brought on a strange fantasy that he hadn't considered much before—him and Violet, in the future, with kids. A family.

The sight made everything even more real. He'd only wanted to make her happy, win her over, take up where their youthful affections had left off...but this?

It overwhelmed him almost to the point of panic.

Had he ever separated himself from the superficial kid he used to be? Or was he still the boy he'd been at eighteen, never progressing emotionally with all his casual dates and his focus on being someone other than a rich kid?

Even worse, it was clear from the way Violet had just reacted to his offer of a shopping spree and makeover that something odd was going on with her. She told him that he was giving her too much, but was that really it?

Was the teenager in him still ultra-aware of Violet's status in this community—the miner's daughter? Had he been attempting to truly make her over so the people in his world would finally accept her?

See? he thought, fear gnawing in his stomach again. *This is what happens when things get serious.* That was why he'd never done serious, especially after being crushed by her the first time.

"Violet," he said, keeping his voice low so he wouldn't wake up the sleeping girl in the other room. "I'm sorry if these gifts make you feel like—"

"—I'm still the girl you have to date in secret?"

It was twisted, but true, and he hadn't even seen it happening until too late.

Maybe he wasn't made for relationships, and that was the bottom line. But even thinking that made his heart rip at the edges.

What had he wanted from Violet?

What did he want now?

He stuck his hands in his jacket pockets, wishing he could take the envelope back. But she was holding onto it tightly.

"Davis, I have to tell you something." She bent the envelope as her hand fisted. "I got a call this morning, from an editor at the *San Francisco Chronicle.*"

He froze. Suddenly it was as if the ceiling was cracking above him, sifting dust and rubble in a prelude to what was to come.

She added, "He wants me to fly out for a job interview."

That's when the ceiling crashed down on him. Not literally, but her announcement had all the impact of that day fifteen years ago when he'd known that they were over. The realization that he didn't mean anything to her and getting out of St. Valentine was so much more important to Violet than he was.

So many warnings, so many times he hadn't listened. Hell, he'd *just* been having doubts about what they were to each other, too.

He should've listened to them....

Violet stepped toward him, dropping the envelope on the floor. "Davis—"

"Do you *want* that job?"

The same pause that had split the air years ago when he'd asked her if she believed his mom's lies forced a chasm between them now. The silence said nothing and everything, even as she answered.

"I *did* want a job just like it," she said, her gaze glassy. "But..." She swallowed, then rushed right on. "But everything changed once I came back. It changed when I let you in, when I realized that I should never have left St. Valentine...or you."

He could only stand there, fear tying him up. And, yeah, he finally could see it as fear, because he'd never expected her to say yes to him, to want more from him than he'd ever given to any other woman.

Did she want him to ask her to stay?

The thought of putting his heart out there for her to take made all the old memories, the anger, come rumbling back.

If she didn't leave now, she was going to sometime. She had done it before when she'd supposedly loved him, so why not now, when they hadn't actually committed to each other yet?

He thought of everything they'd already done wrong—she hadn't yet definitively turned down the job offer, while he was trying to make her over—and he wondered if they were both intent on messing things up before they got too serious.

There was just too much hurt between them. Too much remaining agony for either one of them to ever say something simple like, "Please don't go."

That hurt might *never* go away.

Even Davis knew an excuse when it planted itself in his brain, but it felt like the only thing saving him right now.

His voice was strained when he said, "It might be a good opportunity for you, Vi," and then headed for the door, leaving her before she could leave him this time.

Why?

The question kept bouncing through Violet as she watched him walk away in slow, cold motion, then close the door behind him.

Distantly it occurred to her that she couldn't go after him, deserting Kristy as she slept in the other room. She thought of calling someone at the front desk to see if they could keep an eye on her, but she was still shaking from Davis's response, and she needed a moment.

Or maybe even longer than that.

More questions ricocheted through her as she waited for Rita to return. Would Davis ever be able to get over their past? Was he so far into self-preservation mode that he would never be able to give himself up to her heart and soul?

She'd seen that anger return in him the second she'd told him about the interview in San Francisco, and it had made her panic, because she *did* love him. What they'd found as teenagers had never died and had only been shaped into a new form.

Was it the same for him, though? Or had he given up on her already?

Had it *ever* really been love for him?

When Rita returned from her errands, Violet was still too numb to tell her what had happened. Then, like an automaton, she went down to the saloon to start her shift, hoping the time away from Davis would allow her to come up with answers.

The place was empty during the postlunch lull, and her dad and mom were at the bar with Wiley Scott, talking over lemonades in mason jars. Violet thought she heard the word loan, but before she could be sure, everyone put on smiles, as if that would erase the comment.

But then they took a good look at Violet's face and pulled her over to a seat at the bar.

"What's wrong?" Mom asked.

She *wasn't* going to cry. Nope.

A gush of tears made her turn her face away. "Nothing."

"Nothing, my butt," Dad said while Mom slung an arm around Violet.

Wiley just sat there, seeming awkward as he ran a hand through his silver hair and then drank his lemonade.

It was no use. Holding these emotions in was too much.

"I got a job interview at a paper in San Francisco," she said, her voice wavering.

Out of the corner of her blurred gaze, she saw her parents exchange glances.

Wiley tried to cut the tension by softly patting her on the back. "I knew you could do it. Always did know you'd conquer the world, even back when I owned the *Recorder*."

When Violet couldn't stop the tears, Wiley excused himself, then disappeared.

"It's okay, Vi," Mom said.

"No, it's not. Things didn't go very well with Davis when I told him. And…" Violet fixed her gaze on her mother, who looked so tired with her gray hair in a wilted bun, her eyes slightly red from the extended hours in the grill kitchen.

Dad sat with his beverage, his mouth in that straight, tight line.

"Listen," Mom said. "We know you've gotten… close…to Davis again. You must've told him that you weren't in town for the long run, so didn't he expect an announcement like this?"

Dad interrupted. "I told you I saw the two of them at that dance marathon, and it seemed to me that Violet wasn't about to go anywhere."

Was that the reason her dad hadn't chased off Davis that night or anytime afterward? Because he'd seen what was growing between them and had begun to accept it?

Violet swiped at her wet cheek. "If you're thinking I let Davis believe there was a shot at a future with me..." She sighed heavily. "I *did*. Because I started thinking that maybe we could overcome all our issues."

She'd fallen in love all over again, but she hadn't been brave enough to say it to him. No, she had wanted to *test* him, to see if he would fall to his knees and profess love and ask her to stay first.

But why would he do that when he'd been burned in the past?

Dumb. She'd been so stubborn and dumb.

Dad set down his glass. "Can't you both overcome those issues? Because the last thing I want is to see my little girl crying."

Violet's heart fisted at the care in Dad's voice. "I thought you couldn't stand Davis."

"I wouldn't choose him as my best buddy. But I've never seen you like you are when you're around him, either—happy, excited, content. And I suppose Davis has got good intentions, even if he's..."

It took a lot for her dad to say even that much, and his heartfelt efforts got to her. "Thanks, Dad."

"Thanks for what?"

She didn't know the answer until it clicked into place like a lock that was just about to be freed.

* * *

Davis had sheltered himself in his media and game room, bashing some pool balls into the table pockets with his cue stick. He'd turned on some TVs—one to the business channel with its Wall Street ticker running by, one to a channel that featured mindless repeats of a sitcom he'd never seen before and one on a digital music channel that played country music.

He kept the volume up on that one, blasting noise just so he wouldn't have to listen to his brain screaming at him from different directions about Violet.

She's really going to leave and it'll be your fault.

She's a part of your past.

He slammed the eight ball into a corner pocket so hard that it popped out and thudded onto the carpet.

"You're upset," yelled Lloyd over the music, as he entered the room. He accessed a remote to turn down the volume.

"What makes you think so?"

Davis's assistant was holding a sheaf of papers—no doubt contracts of some sort—but he didn't hand them over yet.

"If I were you," Lloyd said, "I would stay away from the car barn."

"I'm not driving anywhere today."

"That's right, you're going to stay here and murder some balls. I approve. It's far safer."

"Do you want something?" Davis aimed for a striped ball, took his shot, but missed the pocket by a mile.

A curse ripped out of him.

Lloyd, looking so calm and put together in his linen

business shirt, creased gray slacks and slicked dark hair, rested his hip on the table.

"What happened with her today?" he asked.

"Who?"

"You know who I'm talking about."

Davis couldn't even say her name. He was afraid if he did, he would lose what little pride he had left in himself, that he would go right back to her and lay himself out at her mercy, giving her the opportunity to tear him apart all over again.

Instead, he said, "She's probably on her way across the country now for a job interview. And she probably won't ever look back."

"I'm sorry to hear that," Lloyd said, frowning. "She really was far better than your other ladies."

Davis stood up from the shot he was about to take. "She wasn't even in the same category."

From the smug expression on Lloyd's face, Davis could tell that the man had been baiting him.

Dammit. He laid down his cue stick, leaned against the table and released a jagged, pent-up breath. "I was scared to death, Lloyd, and I made sure today that she wasn't going to break me again."

Lloyd and Davis had enjoyed a few cocktails together over the years, so he'd heard the Story of Violet.

"Are you telling me," he said, "that you intended all this time to teach her a lesson by dating her then ditching her?"

"No. It's just that things started to get...deep."

The last word was like a hammer blow, decisive, nailing Davis in place.

"Well," Lloyd said, getting up from the table. "At least you have your pool balls left."

"Small consolation."

"Okay, then. You'll sit here and mope instead. That's far better."

"I'm not moping."

"This, my friend, is the very definition."

As Lloyd left the papers on the table, walking toward the door, Davis said, "So what would you do?"

"Me?" Lloyd shrugged. "I would ask myself if Violet was worth putting my pride on the line."

"It's more than pride." It was everything—his soul, his self-worth.

How had one woman come to own him so completely?

He knew—she was Violet. She was the one who made him laugh and forget the weight that often rested on his shoulders. She was the one who understood his demons and tried, right alongside him, to drive them away.

She was the one he wanted by his side for the rest of his life, even if he had to put his pride and soul at risk.

But would she eventually come to believe that she had given up too much for *him*? One day, would she wake up and regret turning down this job interview based only on a short love affair with an ex-boyfriend?

Lloyd was still watching him, and he smiled.

"I'll drive," he said, leaving the room.

As Davis realized that, all along, there had never been any doubt what he would and should do, he started to roll down his shirtsleeves. His blood raced, drawing him out of the room, racing through the house.

But…the future. He hadn't thought of it before. What would he say besides *I love you* when he got to Violet?

Did it matter right now, just as long as he showed her he wasn't going to let her go without a fight?

He went to the foyer, then opened the front door.

And stood there, shocked.

Chapter Twelve

"Violet." He sounded choked, overcome, as he pulled her into his arms.

In those strong, capable arms, she could feel the future. It was full of days she would never spend wishing she were somewhere else. It was full of knowing that he was and had always been the perfect partner, the perfect fit, and she would never again wonder if there was anything more to life.

He spoke again, his face buried in her hair. "I was on my way over to you to tell you that I love you, Vi. Once I stepped out of that room, I knew I had to go back. But I didn't know how. I *always* loved you."

Something inside of her expanded and filled her. Hope, happiness…

"I love you, too." So easy to say now.

So right.

He smoothed back the hair that had escaped from the ribbon that had been holding it back from her face, and his gaze devoured her, his blue eyes full of emotion.

Now the words tumbled out of her, held back for too long. "I could've taken the easy way out this afternoon. That's what the old me would've done. I would've escaped to the city or somewhere I wouldn't have had to deal with the hurt I always manage to put you through."

"But you stayed."

"There wasn't any other choice—not now. I couldn't stand the thought of a life without you. I wasn't going to make the same mistake I made the first time."

"I would've come after you, no matter where you went." He held her face in his hands.

Her entire body was one heartbeat, and she could feel Davis's through his chest, too. Joined, never to be apart again.

She wrapped him in her arms again, unable to get enough of this, of him.

They stayed like that for what seemed to be hours, but time hardly mattered now. Eventually, though, he kissed her forehead, then lifted her high above him. A laugh burbled out of Violet as Davis twirled her once and she landed in his arms.

They looked into each other's eyes, quiet now, as he carried her across the threshold, shutting the door with his foot, then brought her through the foyer and set her down on the third step on the grand, curved stairway leading to the second floor.

With care, he slipped the ribbon the rest of the way from her hair, and it reminded her of their first true night together, when he'd loosened her hair and it had spread over her shoulders for him to touch, to run his fingers through.

"My Violet," he said softly. "You know I love you just like you are, right? You know that when I bought you those dresses and booked that makeover, I only wanted to show you how I felt. That I wanted to make you feel special. It's only that I wasn't sure how to do that either, and it ended up coming out wrong."

He'd arrived at that realization without her having to spell out how she'd felt about the shopping spree and spa, and a glow spread from the center of her outward.

They would always be able to read each other.

"So," she said, just to be sure, "you weren't making me over so I would be—"

"Like the other women I used to date? I wondered about that, too, until I almost lost you today. No one can even touch you, Vi. No one even comes close."

Tears gathered in her throat, then flooded her eyes.

"I was hoping you'd say that." She ran her fingertips over his cheek, down to his jaw. A tiny thrill buzzed up her hand, her arm, joining the glow in her core. "That's something I'm going to work on—trust. I didn't have any of it after I left St. Valentine, and it was so hard to have it with you when I came back."

"But I'll make sure it's easy for you to have it now."

"Me, too. I never want you to think that I want a job in San Francisco, or that I'm itching to get back to L.A."

"You're not?"

"No." She impulsively kissed him, letting her mouth linger against his as she spoke. "I kept telling myself that

I missed the city, but that was before I knew just what I was going to miss here if I were ever fool enough to leave again."

"I promise I won't do anything that'll make you want to leave."

"I promise that I'm always yours."

He smiled against her lips, then laughed, holding up the ribbon from her hair.

After he wrapped it around her ring finger, then tied it, he said, "Will this work for a promise ring? For the time being, at least?"

She raised her hand, admiring the ribbon, a tear slipping down her cheek. It was the most beautiful ring she'd ever seen because the gesture had come from the very depths of him.

"I told you," she said, "I don't need expensive gifts when I have you."

They kissed again, sealing their promises.

And when Davis scooped her into his arms again, she knew that the ring he'd put on her would always be far more valuable than diamonds or gold.

He was her treasure, forevermore.

Davis carried her up the stairs and into his bedroom, where he set her on her feet then closed the door to the rest of the universe.

As he walked back to her, the sun filtered in through the sliding screen door that led to a balcony, backlighting her so that her hair was a fiery red. She pushed her hair away from her face, and her light brown gaze was shiny, eager, but it wasn't because she didn't know what to expect from him this time.

Thanks to her, he saw everything in a different light—this moment between them, when there would be love instead of just lust. He even saw the world in a better way, because this was the woman who'd given him back his pride. She'd had the power to make him recognize just what he'd done for this town and how much he'd grown from the playboy everyone had expected him to be.

This was the woman who would be his partner, his lover, his everything, and he wanted to savor her in a new way—not just as a guy who was making up for something lost, but as a man who had found exactly who and what he needed.

She slipped off her shoes, kicking them away, and he ran his hands up and down her arms, watching as goose bumps spread across her smooth skin.

"I'm going to do that to every inch of you," he said.

"You already have."

"Vi, we haven't even gotten started."

He rested his hand in the dip between her collarbones, at the base of her throat. As he dragged his hand down between her breasts, it was obvious that he'd excited other parts of her, too, and he cupped her fullness, his thumbs sketching over her nipples.

She bit her lip, closed her eyes, and her reaction sent a shot of heat to his groin.

When he swept his hands lower, to her waist, she reached up to unbutton her top. He stroked his hands to her back, seeking the zipper of her skirt.

She peeled off her top, wiggled out of her skirt, leaving on only her white bra and panties. Her curves made his temperature surge, made him go harder.

He stripped off his shirt then his boots and socks as she unhooked her bra. A hail of clothing hit the ground.

Before she went any further, though, he rested his hands on her hips, caressing her toned stomach with his thumbs.

She held her breath as he lazily traveled his hands up, over her breasts, then explored more of her—down her back, over her rear end. Then he pulled her against him.

When she felt his stiffness, she gasped. And the sound only grew when he coaxed off her panties, bending down so she could step out of them one leg at a time.

He urged her legs apart.

"Oh." The word escaped her—stimulated, anticipating.

He skimmed his hands up her calves to the inside of her thighs, and up even more until his thumbs separated her.

When he kissed her there, she seemed to lose her balance, but he made sure she stayed standing as he loved her, taking pleasure out of how she moaned and grasped his hair, shifting, restless as she winced, cried out a little, then a lot, then—

She shuddered to a climax, and he brought her to the bed, shucking off his jeans.

Against the white of his comforter, she was flushed, her hands threaded through her hair. The tumbled, satiated look of her spiked a fever in him, and he couldn't wait any longer.

He took a condom out of his nightstand drawer, slipping it on, going to Violet's open arms and laying his body over hers.

As he slid into her, she welcomed him as he'd never been welcomed before, surrounded by her in the most intimate embrace. They rocked together in a sultry rhythm that grew more urgent with every moment, tying themselves up in each other like the ribbon he'd wrapped around her finger in an eternal vow.

As he moved in her, he felt cocooned, wrapped more and more... Tangled...lifted...held in the air on a breathtaking pause...

Then, with a rush, he blasted apart, spinning down, unraveling, dizzy—

But just as he thought he would hit the ground hard, he felt her, Violet, holding him, bringing him back together.

Heart to heart.

Soul to soul.

A few days later, the Queen of Hearts was bursting at the seams, full of family and friends as Violet and Davis stood near the bar.

She looked up at him, unable to stop smiling. Every single person in this room knew why they were here, but she'd been dying to make this official announcement, anyway.

Davis held her gaze with his deep blue eyes and smiled, too. Every time he did it, ecstatic shivers consumed her. But there was something else, as well, and it'd been given free rein ever since the other day.

Love.

And it was only going to grow, Violet thought, slipping her hand into his as they faced the crowd. Davis's mother was nowhere to be seen, but Violet spied her parents—Mom wiping at the happy tears in her eyes and Dad with his chin raised, although the hint of a smile played on his mouth. Then there was Rita near the front, with Kristy standing on a chair so she could see as she held onto a brunette, ringlet-haired doll. Wiley Scott was at the bar with a mug of root beer, ready for a toast, as he beamed at his protégés. Even Aaron Rhodes was here, near the back, at a table of women who couldn't keep their eyes off of him.

Other townsfolk had turned out, too, mainly the old-timers Violet had been interviewing for her Tony Amati story. But there were a couple of ex-miners on the fringes, as if they were curious about the ruckus and had wandered in.

Oddest of all, though, was the sight of *the* Jared Colton in the corner of the bar, wearing his black cowboy hat just as low as ever. Violet didn't know if it was purposeful or not, but he was sitting near the picture of Tony Amati that she had shown him that first night.

You can run, Violet thought, *but you can't hide.* She and Davis were going to get to the bottom of his story—and Tony Amati's—yet.

The town she was growing to love a little more each day would be the better for it.

"Thanks for coming," Davis finally said, quieting everyone down.

When the buzz fully settled, he went on, his arm around Violet.

"We're glad you could be here, because there're a couple things we'd like to share."

Aaron loudly cleared his throat, and Violet saw that, not far behind his table, Jennifer Neeson was seated with Lianna Hurst and the mayor, as if they were all buddies now. Interesting times.

"Is it going to take you fifteen more years to make these announcements?" Aaron said.

Laughter filled the room.

Davis laughed, too. "There's nobody who's been waiting longer than the two of us."

As everyone applauded, Davis gave Violet another hug, then a kiss that drew even more approval.

"Anyhow," Davis said, as he kept his gaze on Violet, then reluctantly dragged it away, "there's more of a civic announcement we'd like to make first. Most of you are familiar with the old Hamill property just outside St. Valentine. You know it's been deserted for quite a while, but we'd like to put it to good use as a sort of town project."

The room stilled as Davis outlined what he and Violet had talked about that sunny day at the ranch, just before they'd made love for the first time since she'd returned. He talked about jobs for St. Valentine, a ranch where disadvantaged kids could interact with and raise horses, a glimmer of hope for so many who needed it.

Applause met the announcement until Davis held up his hand. "There's more."

Violet couldn't wait another second, and she held up

her hand, showing everyone the simple, elegant diamond ring on her finger. It was twined in a beautiful rope that would never undo itself.

And that was when all control in the room crumbled. Wiley and Rita rushed up to them, congratulating and hugging them. More townspeople took their turns, too. Little Kristy was delighted when it came time to embrace Violet, and she had the new couple hug her doll, too. Even the people whom Violet didn't think gave a fig about her seemed sincerely happy, and when she caught Davis's eye, he saw how satisfied he was that she had finally come home.

And that he had found a true one in her, too.

When Davis announced that drinks were on the house, there was even more of a clamor toward the bar, and she was separated from him, pulled away by Rita.

Right away she felt as if she was missing an important part of herself. Out of the corner of her gaze she saw Aaron Rhodes slapping Davis on the back, laughing with his friend.

Rita used her hand to guide Violet's focus back to her. "There're other people in the room, you know."

"Sorry."

Laughing, Rita gave her another big hug. "I can't believe it. The infamous Violet and Davis finally worked it out. I'm so happy for you."

She had said it a little too giddily, and there was a strange blush on Rita's cheeks.

Something was up.

Violet narrowed her gaze at her, asking without asking, and Rita glanced over at Kristy to check on her.

She shouldn't have bothered, because Wiley was entertaining the girl with the doll.

Rita pulled Violet toward the back of the restaurant, in the hallway near the grill where there was relative quiet.

"What's going on?" Violet asked.

Rita gave her a massive grin and looked as if she were about to explode.

She'd never seen her friend this way, not even when Kevin, her own first love and the man who'd eventually run off on her, had asked Rita out on her first date in high school.

"It finally happened for me," she said.

"What?"

"Love."

Violet widened her eyes. "Wow. I…" She squeezed her friend's hands. "That's great. Who…? How…?"

"Last night. He was passing through town on a business trip and… Vi, I know I don't usually do these kinds of things, but it just happened. And he's the one. I know it more than I've ever known anything."

Whoa. Rita was probably the most careful woman around. She'd been hurt just as much as Violet and Davis in the past. Besides that, she was incredibly mindful of Kristy and her feelings about bringing another man into the picture.

It was bad enough that Rita had grown up in this town with the reputation of being dumped and pregnant, so she'd always kept to herself. But this?

Whoa.

Rita rushed on. "He had to leave this morning, but he's going to be back, after he takes care of some ranching business." She smiled again, absolutely glowing. "I never believed in love at first sight, but there was something about him that made me change my mind. It's almost a…"

"Miracle?"

"Yes."

Violet wouldn't argue with that. "What's his name?"

"Conn Flannigan. He was in the bar last night."

Violet hadn't been working, but she wished she'd been there. Dammit. She had a bad feeling about this.

Had Rita lost her head? It was one thing for Violet to have gotten back together with an old boyfriend, but this Conn guy was a stranger.

Just as she was about to ask her friend a load of questions, Violet's mom found them.

"There you are. You've got to see this."

Violet gave Rita a helpless glance as Mom pulled her out of the hallway, and Rita just shrugged in an it's-okay-we'll-talk-later way.

Yeah, they *would* talk. That was for sure.

Once out in the main room, Mom pointed toward the bar, where Davis was sitting next to…

Dad?

"Tell me this is a good thing," Violet said.

Mom patted her arm. "He's just congratulating him. Your father's going to be one hundred percent fine about this, Vi. It took a bit for him to let go of his little girl, but Davis has a good heart. Dad really does believe that."

When Dad heartily shook Davis's hand, then left the bar, Violet smiled at Mom, then went to her future husband.

"Now," she said, holding his hand, "we'll wait for your mother to show up."

"Right," Davis said. "Maybe that could happen eventually. If she doesn't come around, though, I don't see how she'll expect a relationship with me." He kissed her. "You're my life, my will-be wife...my everything."

Violet kissed him back. "You're everything to me, too."

And as the people of St. Valentine laughed and came together, even in this small way, Davis and Violet wrapped their arms around each other.

Never letting go.

* * * * *

*Look for the next book in Crystal Green's
new miniseries,*
ST. VALENTINE, TEXAS
Coming soon, wherever Harlequin books are sold.

HEART & HOME

Heartwarming romances where love can
happen right when you least expect it.

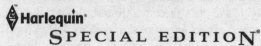

SPECIAL EDITION®

COMING NEXT MONTH
AVAILABLE MAY 29, 2012

#2191 FORTUNE'S PERFECT MATCH
The Fortunes of Texas: Whirlwind Romance
Allison Leigh

#2192 ONCE UPON A MATCHMAKER
Matchmaking Mamas
Marie Ferrarella

#2193 THE RANCHER'S HIRED FIANCÉE
Brighton Valley Babies
Judy Duarte

#2194 THE CAMDEN COWBOY
Northbridge Nuptials
Victoria Pade

#2195 AN OFFICER, A BABY AND A BRIDE
The Foster Brothers
Tracy Madison

#2196 NO ORDINARY JOE
Michelle Celmer

REQUEST YOUR FREE BOOKS!

2 FREE NOVELS PLUS 2 FREE GIFTS!

♦ Harlequin®

SPECIAL EDITION

Life, Love & Family

YES! Please send me 2 FREE Harlequin® Special Edition novels and my 2 FREE gifts (gifts are worth about $10). After receiving them, if I don't wish to receive any more books, I can return the shipping statement marked "cancel." If I don't cancel, I will receive 6 brand-new novels every month and be billed just $4.49 per book in the U.S. or $5.24 per book in Canada. That's a saving of at least 14% off the cover price! It's quite a bargain! Shipping and handling is just 50¢ per book in the U.S. and 75¢ per book in Canada.* I understand that accepting the 2 free books and gifts places me under no obligation to buy anything. I can always return a shipment and cancel at any time. Even if I never buy another book, the two free books and gifts are mine to keep forever.

235/335 HDN FEGF

Name	(PLEASE PRINT)	
Address		Apt. #
City	State/Prov.	Zip/Postal Code

Signature (if under 18, a parent or guardian must sign)

Mail to the Reader Service:
IN U.S.A.: P.O. Box 1867, Buffalo, NY 14240-1867
IN CANADA: P.O. Box 609, Fort Erie, Ontario L2A 5X3

Not valid for current subscribers to Harlequin Special Edition books.

Want to try two free books from another line?
Call 1-800-873-8635 or visit www.ReaderService.com.

* Terms and prices subject to change without notice. Prices do not include applicable taxes. Sales tax applicable in N.Y. Canadian residents will be charged applicable taxes. Offer not valid in Quebec. This offer is limited to one order per household. All orders subject to credit approval. Credit or debit balances in a customer's account(s) may be offset by any other outstanding balance owed by or to the customer. Please allow 4 to 6 weeks for delivery. Offer available while quantities last.

Your Privacy—The Reader Service is committed to protecting your privacy. Our Privacy Policy is available online at www.ReaderService.com or upon request from the Reader Service.

We make a portion of our mailing list available to reputable third parties that offer products we believe may interest you. If you prefer that we not exchange your name with third parties, or if you wish to clarify or modify your communication preferences, please visit us at www.ReaderService.com/consumerchoice or write to us at Reader Service Preference Service, P.O. Box 9062, Buffalo, NY 14269. Include your complete name and address.

HSE11B

Harlequin

SPECIAL EDITION

Life, Love and Family

USA TODAY bestselling author

Marie Ferrarella

enchants readers in

ONCE UPON A MATCHMAKER

Micah Muldare's aunt is worried that her nephew is going to wind up alone in his old age...but this matchmaking mama has just the thing! When Micah finds himself accused of theft, defense lawyer Tracy Ryan agrees to help him as a favor to his aunt, but soon finds herself drawn to more than just his case. Will Micah open up his heart and realize Tracy is his match?

MATCHMAKING *Mamas*

Available June 2012

Saddle up with Harlequin® series books this summer and find a cowboy for every mood!

Available wherever books are sold.

www.Harlequin.com

HSE65674

*A grim discovery is about to change everything for
Detective Layne Sullivan—including how she
interacts with her boss!*

*Read on for an exciting excerpt of the upcoming book
UNRAVELING THE PAST by Beth Andrews....*

SOMETHING WAS UP—otherwise why would Chief Ross
Taylor summon her back out? As Detective Layne Sullivan
walked over, she grudgingly admitted he was doing well.
But that didn't change the fact that the Chief position
should have been hers.

Taylor turned as she approached. "Detective Sullivan,
we have a situation."

"What's the problem?"

He aimed his flashlight at the ground. The beam illumi-
nated a dirt-encrusted skull.

"Definitely a problem." And not something she'd expected. Not here. "How'd you see it?"

"Jess stumbled upon it looking for her phone."

Layne looked to where his niece huddled on a log. "I'll
contact the forensics lab."

"Already have a team on the way. I've also called in units
to search for the rest of the remains."

So he'd started the ball rolling. Then, she'd assume command while he took Jess home. "I have this under control."

Though it was late, he was clean shaven and neat, his flat
stomach a testament to his refusal to indulge in doughnuts.
His dark blond hair was clipped at the sides, the top long
enough to curl.

The female part of Layne admitted he was attractive.

The cop in her resented the hell out of him for it.

"You get a lot of missing-persons cases here?" he asked.

"People don't go missing from Mystic Point." Although plenty of them left. "But we have our share of crime."

"I'll take the lead on this one."

Bad enough he'd come to *her* town and taken the position she was meant to have, now he wanted to mess with *how* she did her job? "Why? I'm the only detective on third shift and your second in command."

"Careful, Detective, or you might overstep."

But she'd never played it safe.

"I don't think it's overstepping to clear the air. You have something against me?"

"I assign cases based on experience and expertise. You don't have to like how I do that, but if you need to question every decision, perhaps you'd be happier somewhere else."

"Are you threatening my job?"

He moved so close she could feel the warmth from his body. "I'm not threatening anything." His breath caressed her cheek. "I'm giving you the choice of what happens next."

What will Layne choose? Find out in
UNRAVELING THE PAST by Beth Andrews,
available June 2012 from Harlequin® Superromance®.

And be sure to look for the other two books
in Beth's THE TRUTH ABOUT THE SULLIVANS series
available in August and October 2012.

Harlequin *Romance*

A touching new duet from fan-favorite author

SUSAN MEIER

First Time **D A D S !**

When millionaire CEO Max Montgomery spots
Kate Hunter-Montgomery—the wife he's never forgotten—
back in town with a daughter who looks just like him, he's
determined to win her back. But can this savvy business tycoon
convince Kate to trust him a second time with her heart?

Find out this June in

THE TYCOON'S SECRET DAUGHTER

And look for book 2 coming this August!

NANNY FOR THE MILLIONAIRE'S TWINS

Saddle up with Harlequin® series books this summer
and find a cowboy for every mood!

Harlequin®

INTRIGUE

USA TODAY **BESTSELLING AUTHOR**

B.J.Daniels

CAPTIVATES WITH ANOTHER INSTALLMENT OF

∻ WHITEHORSE ∾
MONTANA

Chisholm Cattle Company

It's a strange event when Zane Chisholm finds a beautiful
woman on his doorstep. A series of even stranger events
follow, including Dakota Lansing showing up in search of the
unknown woman. Dakota is a childhood friend who has had
a crush on Zane since she was a kid. Now they find themselves
working together to solve the mystery…which is bigger
than they first suspected!

WRANGLED

Available June 2012

Saddle up with Harlequin® series books this
summer and find a cowboy for every mood!

Available wherever books are sold.

HI69620